Zack wanted the
Skin to skin.

And when they were, he lifted Victoria onto the bar, placing her so she was facing the huge mirror. Golden candlelight flickered in the dusky saloon and the reflection of their naked bodies bathed in the glow was erotic and compelling. With one hand he began exploring her while she watched in fascination.

When she began to moan, he manoeuvred her until she was face down on the bar.

His expert massage was not meant to relax her at all. His devilish laughter gave him away as he worked magic with his hands, kneading and rubbing and working his way down her back, past her waist. He knew exactly the effect he was causing when his hands cupped her bottom and squeezed.

'I want to turn over,' came Victoria's muffled, tortured voice.

'Not yet,' he said, continuing to fuel her pleasure. Tonight they were going to do things *his* way, and he wanted to prove to her that he was the good guy. The *really* good guy. At least, with his hands.

Dear Reader,

One of my greatest joys in life is making cute guys blush. I love to tease in the very best sense of the word. My favourite dance is the tango. It's suggestive, with those slinky clothes and attitude to spare. It's dancing on the edge. It's that edge I love.

I adore writing sexy books for the same reason. It's a little naughty—like being the only girl in a detention room full of bad boys. Somehow that never seemed like punishment to me, so I didn't learn my lesson about not writing make-believe notes so my friends could skip school. I eventually realized the life of the writer was for me—I could justify sleeping in, warm in bed and daydreaming—so I settled on a career as a voyeur. Temptation® has always let me go past the bedroom door with my characters. Now BLAZE lets me go even farther.

Hope you'll come with me for a walk on the wild side.

Sincerely,

Tiffany White

———— ❦ ————

To Lance Thomure, who made sure we saw every ghost town from St. Louis to Colorado Springs... even the one in the sky.

To Nikki Benjamin, author of *Restless Winds* (one good fantasy deserves another!)

And for my editor, Susan Sheppard, who knows her way around the seductive dance of fantasy.

RESTLESS NIGHTS

BY

TIFFANY WHITE

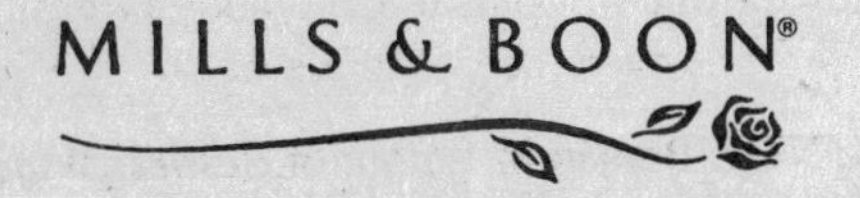

DID YOU PURCHASE THIS BOOK WITHOUT A COVER?

If you did, you should be aware it is **stolen property** as it was reported *unsold and destroyed* by a retailer. Neither the author nor the publisher has received any payment for this book.

All the characters in this book have no existence outside the imagination of the author, and have no relation whatsoever to anyone bearing the same name or names. They are not even distantly inspired by any individual known or unknown to the author, and all the incidents are pure invention.

All Rights Reserved including the right of reproduction in whole or in part in any form. This edition is published by arrangement with Harlequin Enterprises II B.V. The text of this publication or any part thereof may not be reproduced or transmitted in any form or by any means, electronic or mechanical, including photocopying, recording, storage in an information retrieval system, or otherwise, without the written permission of the publisher.

This book is sold subject to the condition that it shall not, by way of trade or otherwise, be lent, resold, hired out or otherwise circulated without the prior consent of the publisher in any form of binding or cover other than that in which it is published and without a similar condition including this condition being imposed on the subsequent purchaser.

*MILLS & BOON and MILLS & BOON with the Rose Device are registered trademarks of the publisher.
TEMPTATION is a registered trademark of Harlequin Enterprises Limited, used under licence.*

*First published in Great Britain 1998
by Harlequin Mills & Boon Limited,
Eton House, 18-24 Paradise Road, Richmond, Surrey TW9 1SR*

© Anna Eberhardt

ISBN 0 263 80808 4

21-9802

*Printed and bound in Great Britain
by Caledonian International Book Manufacturing Ltd, Glasgow*

1

VICTORIA STONE PARKED her car in the gravel lot beside Desperado's, the country-and-western saloon her fiancé, Paul Brooks, owned. Her hand on the steering wheel looked bare without the engagement ring that usually sparkled there. She had wrenched the ring off and left it at home on her dressing table when Paul had called to break their date for the evening. He'd cancelled at the last minute again, sure she would understand because it was business.

He was wrong. As far as she was concerned their engagement was off until they had a little talk.

The marriage and children she wanted demanded a good provider, and Paul was that. She had agreed to marry him because he was dependable and safe. Still, she didn't want to be taken for granted. She knew Paul loved her, and that should be enough. Fireworks weren't going to happen for her, but that was reality.

It hadn't occurred to her until tonight that maybe Paul had chosen *her* because she was safe. With her as his wife he could concentrate on his business and she would understand. She knew it didn't make any sense for her to be angry at Paul for doing exactly the same thing she'd done, but she was.

And if he had chosen her because she was safe, he'd made a mistake. Lately she didn't feel safe at all—her emotions were near the surface and explosive.

She stalked into Desperado's, ready for a fight.

Once inside, she managed to get a good table with a view of the band, playing on a low platform next to the bar. After exchanging pleasantries with the waitress, she settled back in her chair and sipped the strawberry margarita she'd ordered, watching the dancers circle counterclockwise around the dance floor. No one approached her—her body language warned them away.

Her gaze turned to the closed door of Paul's office. The band had announced the last song before they took a break. If Paul wasn't out here by the time the band finished the song, she was leaving.

She scanned the sea of blue jeans and cowboy boots at the bar. Absently, she perused the broad shoulders in plaid flannel shirts, the hard thighs in tight denim, the big work-hardened hands wrapped around long-necked bottles of beer. She didn't bother to look above the men's collars. Finally, her gaze came to rest on the last figure at the bar; he was standing not ten feet from where she sat.

Hmm...interesting. Low-heeled boots of black suede instead of cowboy boots. And snug black pants tucked into those boots. Long muscular thighs. Her gaze traveled to his hands, which were slightly large for his body, hands with a disturbing sensuality. The close-fitting black T-shirt tucked in at his narrow waist revealed a hard, flat stomach that only served to emphasize the package below it, which was producing a warm tingling....

Suddenly, she was in a fragrant southern garden with a desperado's gloved hand clamped roughly over her soft mouth. Her struggle was hindered by her full satin ball gown as she twisted violently in his grasp, furiously trying to escape him, only to hear his rich chuckle of amusement when her struggle brought the curve of her breast into contact with his other hand. A hand he had the audacity to let linger in a perverse caress before wrapping his strong arm around her slender waist and easily pinning her against him.

The sounds of laughter and music floating into the garden from the stately house grew fainter as he drew her deeper into the lush, fragrant garden. When he was satisfied they were hidden from view, he turned her in his arms, dragging his gloved hand from her tender mouth. His dark eyes dared her to scream, while an arrogant smile slanted across his lips and he pulled her without subtlety against his lean, hard length, then bent and crushed his mouth to hers.

Her passive response was not to his liking and his kiss grew more insistent, more coaxing. When her body finally betrayed her, causing her lips to part of their own accord, she could feel his mouth forming a satisfied smile beneath her own. She was startled out of her sensual lassitude by the whinny of a horse nearby. The stranger did not heed it, but she began to struggle anew, recoiling in alarm when her slender hand brushed against the cold steel pistol strapped low on his thigh. The horse whinnied again....

Victoria came back to reality with a jolt and realized there was a cellular phone ringing at the next table; its owner was at the bar. When the ringing stopped, she mused about the fantasy the phone had interrupted.

It was always the same. The scene varied, but the theme was always the same—always a dark stranger forcing her to acknowledge the passionate nature she repressed in reality. Always he wore a gun strapped to his lean hard thigh.

This had been going on for months, since she'd begun planning a vacation of visiting ghost towns. Western lore had always fascinated her, in particular the lone gunslinger. At first she'd been amused by her erotic imaginings, but that amusement had long since vanished. She was slipping into the fantasy with alarming frequency. It was becoming spontaneous, uncontrolled. Would she soon have trouble distinguishing fantasy from reality? A trickle of fear slithered down her spine.

This time, it had been the man in black who'd triggered the fantasy.

He was obviously new to Desperado's. He was out of place, but his masculine grace was more virile than all the bolts of denim in the St. Louis saloon. Although his appearance drew sidelong glances, he had a presence about him that deterred challenge.

The band's supposed last song before break turned into two with the beginning strains of a slow, seductive wanting song. She was afraid to look at the stranger. She knew she was being a coward as she kept her eyes on his belt.

But she was also tired of being ignored. Her anger emboldened her to make eye contact with danger. She raised her glass to her lips to empty it, and as she tilted her head back to swallow, her gaze moved up from the stranger's body to his face.

Smoldering dark eyes were waiting for her, their soft pupils telling her that he'd been watching her study him and that his thoughts had been equally erotic.

She watched in fascinated dread as he pushed away from the bar and moved toward her, his dark eyes never once leaving her face. She was unable to move, though her mind argued with her body, demanding flight. It wasn't until he reached her that she realized she'd been holding her breath, and exhaled in a breathy rush. Refusal was not an option when he placed his hand firmly in the center of her back and led her to the dance floor. The added height of her boots brought them into intimate contact when he pulled her close. Everywhere their bodies touched became warm and feverish, her face against the dark stubble of his square jaw most of all.

The crush of people on the dimly lit dance floor contributed to the sensuality and warmth emanating between them. The entire surface of her body became a receptor of pleasure as they swayed gently against each other. A bead of sweat slid from his jaw when he finally pulled his head back to look down at her. She was going up in flames and fancied she saw them reflected in his eyes as he looked into hers, telling her that he knew. *He knew!*

When he leaned closer and his mouth opened against the side of her bare neck, she gasped involuntarily. A sudden, hot weakness flashed in her belly, settling with a moist ache between her thighs. His lips whispered a caress along her hairline as he slid trembling hands up over her ribs, burning a path through her soft cotton sweater, his thumbs barely grazing the curves of her breasts before returning to rest at her waist.

Her arms were around his neck, and she was unable and unwilling to stop him when he slid his fingers into the back pockets of her jeans, drawing her intimately up against the full hardness of his arousal. Using the knowledge her eyes had given him, he began applying the subtlest of pressure, moving her in a tantalizingly slow circular motion against him.

She was out of control and weak with desire, her breath coming in pants, the inside of her thighs clenching in anticipation. In the crowd of dancers no one could see that what they were doing had little to do with dancing.

All this time he had been moving her against him, until at last, seeming to lose himself for a moment, he thrust against her. A low, strangled groan escaped his lips, pressed against her ear. Shiveringly erotic, the sound reverberated within her, rushing to her loins. Like a raindrop sliding down a windowpane, it gathered momentum along the way, triggering the explosion of passion that had been building to an unbearable pitch inside her. She jerked against him, then tried to pull away. He refused to allow it, his strong hand pressing her body in close to his, while his other hand stroked her hair, gentling her. She knew he could feel the shudders of her orgasm as she bit her lips to keep from crying out. She kept her eyes closed, refusing to look at him as she heard the song end.

THE BONE-CRACKING SOUND of a fist connecting signaled the outbreak of a free-for-all on the dance floor. Victoria seized her chance for escape when a falling body separated them and her partner was drawn into the spirited Friday-night brawl. With a wild grab she nabbed the purse she'd left on the table and fled outside to the parking lot, her mind filled with self-recrimination. What was wrong with her? She'd never done anything like that before in her life. While her fantasies may have gotten a little out of hand on occasion, in real life she was very much a lady.

Her boots crunched on the loose gravel as she ran for her car, and in her haste she stumbled and lost her balance, dropping her purse and spilling its contents.

She cursed her clumsiness as she knelt to search for her things in the darkness. She had recovered everything, even spotting her keys glimmering in the moonlight, when she had the disquieting feeling she was no longer alone in the deserted parking lot. She made a desperate grab for her keys, only to jump back with a sharp, indrawn breath when they were covered by a man's booted foot. A black suede boot, she noticed with both relief and despair.

"I guess this means you don't want to go somewhere and talk about it." His voice flowed, slow and smooth as syrup, as he dropped down beside her. She was no longer afraid, yet her heart was pounding. Why didn't he just leave her alone?

"T-talk...about what?" she stammered.

"About what just happened," he answered. His lean face, all planes and angles, was just inches from hers, the short stubble of his dark beard lending him a ruthless handsomeness as he watched her with knowing eyes.

"Nothing happened!" she rasped in denial, fighting for air, drowning in the soft blackness of his eyes.

"*Liar.*" His voice was low with mockery. He shifted

his weight on the balls of his feet and drew the back of his fingertips along her jaw to emphasize his point. He didn't so much as move an inch toward her while he waited, yet the space between them seemed to evaporate.

"Just leave it!" she begged frantically as she jumped up in desperation. He rose beside her, his strong hand encircling her dainty wrist. She looked down at her hand captured in his and shivered at what the physical contact was doing to her insides. She looked back up at him, fighting the desire she felt as she met his eyes. "Please," she murmured.

His dark eyes searched hers, sorting, deciding. "You're sure...?" he demanded.

"Yes," she answered at last, her eyes downcast.

He turned her slender hand over and dropped her keys in her palm. Then he wrapped her fingers over the keys and brought her fist to his mouth. With erotic insinuation, his lips and tongue played gently over each knuckle. It was only at the last knuckle that he betrayed his hunger and let his teeth bite down and rake her skin. The action sent tremors of desire pulsing through her.

His voice was low as he watched her from beneath sensuous, heavy lids. "I'm only in St. Louis for a week. I'll be here at Desperado's every night, waiting...should you find the courage." He released her hand then and turned and walked back to the saloon, where for one brief moment he was silhouetted in the doorway: dark, lean and as lethal as a gunslinger.

He disappeared inside and she turned to her car, fumbling with the key until she calmed down enough to unlock the door. Her hands shook all the way home. When she pulled into her driveway, she sat for a moment with her forehead resting on her arms, crossed over the steering wheel. Finally, she let herself into the house and headed for her bedroom. Tossing her keys and purse on the bed, she sank down on the vanity bench in front of her dressing table, her thoughts a jumble.

What on earth had possessed her? The man who'd held her in his arms on the dance floor, taking the liberties she'd allowed, had been a total stranger, and yet she'd been unable to control her actions. Moreover, she'd welcomed his. She'd welcomed his caresses and acted so unlike herself that there had been two strangers to her on the dance floor tonight.

What must he think of her? And her fiancé, Paul, had been right there in his office. What if his meeting had ended and he'd opened his door to see her? This wasn't a harmless fantasy like the others, this was reality, and it scared her to death. Yet she'd never felt anything so strongly before. It was like being drugged; once the feeling swept over her body, she'd had no control over its effect. She'd never gone up in flames like that for anyone. She'd imagined that the stranger had felt the same way, too, but her sense of reality was becoming distorted and she couldn't be sure.

She got up and took a shower, wanting to wash away the smell of him, which was haunting her. But it only made matters worse, because everywhere she slid the soapy sponge was a reminder of his body touching hers. She had been both sated and aroused beyond any previous experience by what had happened. After she finished toweling off, she slipped into bed...but not to sleep.

She couldn't get the stranger out of her mind. Had there been just the hint of a cruel smile when he'd looked into her eyes and known what she was feeling? A smile of absolute confidence that he could deliver what she wanted—needed? And hadn't he done more than just promise, with both of them fully clothed in a room full of people? What would have happened if she'd been alone with him? No, better not to think of that.

Her eyes blinked wide open. My god, she didn't even know his name. If he hadn't followed her to the parking lot, she wouldn't have even spoken one word to him...out loud.

Well, she'd never see him again. He had said he was only in town for a week and she would be out of town all week. She and Paul had been planning this drive to Colorado for months. A week away from everything was just what she needed—now more than ever. She'd been working too hard. Yes, that was the problem.

Her business as a personal shopper had grown to the point where she really did need to think about hiring someone to help her. She'd rushed to accommodate all her clients before she left on her trip. That meant reading the extensive files she kept on each of them as to their tastes, measurements, career and personal requirements. She had to know what each store in town carried in inventory and to maintain relationships with the store employees so she knew in advance of any new shipments or sales.

By the time a customer called she already pretty much knew what she would need and where she could locate it. But the constant legwork was taking a toll. When she returned from her trip she would hire someone to help her. Besides, when she married Paul—if she married Paul—she'd want to focus more of her time on the family she wanted.

Feeling better, she fell into a restful sleep until the shrill ring of her alarm clock woke her early Saturday morning. She flung out her arm and turned off the clock automatically.

Stretching sleepily, she rubbed her eyes, not wanting to get out of bed. She walked barefoot to the closet to slide into a silk kimono, because she never remembered to close the shutters at the kitchen window and didn't wish to scandalize her neighbors.

After she tied the sash securely at her small waist, she headed for the kitchen and a cold can of cola from the refrigerator. Paul cringed every time he saw her start the morning with soda. He refused to agree with her that caffeine was caffeine no matter if it came from coffee or a can of cola.

She took a swig, enjoying the slight acidity of the cold drink as it slid down her throat.

The cola served its purpose and began to wake her up. She was a deep sleeper, a deep sleeper prone to lots of dreaming. Especially when things were rushed. It seemed that her imagination, which helped her be so good at her job, couldn't be turned off.

And then she gulped as she remembered last night's dream. Or was it real? No! No...it must have been a dream. Her dreams were like that. They always seemed so real. It was funny how dreams allowed you to do things you'd never think of doing in reality. Imagine dancing like that with a total stranger. With anyone, for that matter. It wasn't as if she was extroverted and totally at ease with people. On the contrary, she was often mistaken for a snob because her shyness looked like aloofness. She grinned and shook her head. It was a good thing Paul couldn't read her mind. He would be thoroughly shocked by the fantasies of his "shy" fiancée.

She'd begun to fantasize as a young girl. It had been lonely being an only child. Her father was always busy working and her mother was a serious woman with no inclination to laughter or affection. There were no bright colors or strong emotions in their home. To make up for the lack of stimulation, Victoria began fantasizing about the places and people she read about in books. It was a simple, harmless way to bring pleasure and color into her drab childhood. Now, as an adult, it was a part of her. Except lately her fantasies had become decidedly erotic.

Victoria blushed as she remembered last night's dream.

The bird Paul had given her for her birthday suddenly squawked from the corner by the kitchen window. If it had been up to her, she would have preferred something smooth and sleek like a kitten for a pet, but Racket had won her over with his ornery personality. She uncaged him, and he had just swooped down to rest on her shoulder when the phone rang.

"Hi," she answered cheerfully.

"Hi, babe. Missed you last night. It's just as well you didn't make it. Things got kinda hectic around here. There was a fight, and I'm spending my time clearing up the mess. Why don't you come over and we can get lunch later?"

"Give me an hour, okay? I'll have to stop on the way to pick up some food for Racket. You want anything?"

"No. I can do without breakfast from a pet-food store. And don't bring me one of your ghastly granola bars, either. I'll never understand your diet of half health food and half junk food. However, and I don't know why, I'll let you choose where we have lunch," he offered.

"Deal," she accepted.

"Okay, babe, see you in about an hour. Bye."

Victoria went to the bedroom to dress, and Racket flew from her shoulder to the saucer of water she'd placed in front of the dressing-table mirror for the bird. Racket began taking a bath, showering the mirror with droplets as he ruffled his feathers and flirted with his reflection.

Victoria dressed in a tank top, walking shorts and an oversize shirt in an island print, thinking it might be a little cool yet this early in the day. Racket flew over to perch on her head, which she hated, and he knew it. He watched Victoria pull on her sandals, nearly toppling as he hastily crawled down her neck each time she bent forward. Finally he gave up his game and flew back to the dressing table to peck kisses at himself in the mirror.

Victoria herself peered into the mirror. She had acquired a biscuit-colored tan and decided she needed only a touch of mascara. Racket strolled between the crystal perfume bottles, watching her as she pulled her hair into a ponytail that changed her appearance from womanly to girlish. He put up a squawk when she put him back in the cage, but she pacified him with a treat, then grabbed a chocolate-chip granola bar for herself on the way out, thinking Paul might not feel like giving her lunch after they had their little talk about his taking her for granted. She opened her purse and retrieved her engagement ring. It sparkled in the sunlight as she slid it on her finger. She might have overreacted when she'd taken it off last night, but she wasn't going to let Paul charm her into being reasonable.

Paul Brooks could charm the paint off a wall. His conventional good looks and ready smile gave him the earnest appearance of a rising young politician, though his interests lay in business for now. Last week, after two years of trying, he had finally worn down her resistance, convincing her that she could no longer afford to wait for the elusive knight in shining armor. Paul had grinned, cinching his argument with, "Besides, who do you think gets to polish all that blasted armor to keep it shining once you're married?"

Okay, so he was right. She didn't *really* believe in the fantasy of romance and happy ever after, but without it everything seemed such a cheat.

Paul was an easy choice. Decent and practical, he was exactly the sort of man she needed, one with his feet planted firmly on the ground. That could be very appealing to a woman who was beginning to worry that her rich fantasy life was starting to overshadow reality. While always before she had been in control of her fantasies, lately she had the uneasy feeling they were controlling her.

It was a beautiful sunny day as Victoria backed out of her driveway. When she stopped at a light she popped open the roof of her car and turned on the radio, which was tuned to country music. No, she wasn't in the mood for country for some reason. She switched it over to rock. By the time she got to Desperado's she was in a great mood. She guessed it was the excitement one always feels before leaving on vacation. It had been a struggle, but Paul had finally agreed he could let a friend run the saloon for one week and take care of the bird. She had the feeling it was mainly because he didn't want her driving alone to Colorado and stopping at the ghost towns that fascinated her along the way. Ghost towns weren't Paul's idea of a good time. He liked people and action.

Paul was in his office when Victoria walked into the saloon. Desperado's was so different in daylight. It always amazed her how bright and sleepy it was with none of the nuances the night brings. Paul got up and came around the front of his desk to greet her with a hug. "Just finished sweeping up," he said, giving her a perfunctory kiss. "Babe, I've got someone here I want you to meet."

Victoria noticed for the first time that there was someone else in the room. He had his back to them and was studying the bulletin board on the wall. "Zack, old buddy, I want you to meet my fiancée, Victoria Stone." On hearing his name, Zack turned, and Victoria's heart plummeted to her feet as her eyes widened in recognition.

A slow, cynical smile slanted across Zack's lips as he offered his hand to Victoria. "So...this is your sweet, shy Victoria you've been telling me so much about."

Victoria just stood there speechless, giving testimony to Paul's description of her. The look in Zack's eyes said he wasn't buying. And she didn't blame him. It was *him!* She supposed she deserved the mocking assessment in his eyes.

Unaware of the tension between Victoria and Zack, Paul continued, "Zack is my best friend from back home. We don't get to see much of each other because he's a Hollywood stuntman, but he's promised to be here for our wedding, whenever we set the date, and to be my best man."

Now would be a good time to beam me aboard, Scotty, Victoria thought whimsically, wanting to disappear as fear and embarrassment warred for the upper hand in her mind. Last night she'd overstepped the boundary of fantasy. Last night *had* been all too real. Zack wasn't a figment of her imagination, he was the man she'd "danced" with last night. The electricity traveling between her hand and Zack's was so intense she was surprised Paul couldn't hear the crackle. And Zack was enjoying every minute of her discomfort as she managed finally to croak out a strangled, "Nice to meet you...er...ah...Zack."

"*My* pleasure, Victoria," Zack said, his voice caressing her name purposefully while he held her right hand a beat longer than was polite. Dropping it at last, he slid his gaze to her left hand and smiled sardonically at the large diamond twinkling on her ring finger. The diamond hadn't been there last night when he'd taken her into his arms. She had been so angry with Paul she hadn't worn it. But that wasn't what it looked like. It looked like deceit, and the cold black eyes appraising her told her what kind of woman he thought his best friend was making the mistake of his life with.

Zack looked up from her ring finger and his gaze lingered on her face. There was challenge in his dark eyes as he said, "Funny, I have the strangest feeling that we've met before. Eyes like yours would be hard to forget." His own eyes told her it wasn't her eyes he was remembering.

Anger replaced embarrassment as Victoria battled his arrogance with her reply. "No, I'm sure you and I haven't been properly introduced."

Zack inclined his head in a silent touché as he moved away.

Paul came forward and slid his arm around Victoria's waist. "I'm afraid I'm not going to be able to make the trip to Colorado with you, so you'll have to postpone it. The men I met with last night want to franchise Desperado's, and the deal they're offering is too good to pass up. There are all kinds of legal details to be worked out and I have to be here."

"But honey, you know how I've been looking forward to this trip for months. I've rearranged my schedule twice to fit yours. I can't rearrange it again. Please, Paul, I need this trip," she coaxed with a peck on his cheek.

Paul colored at her show of affection. "Sorry, babe."

"Then I'll go alone." Victoria pouted prettily, stepping away.

"Now, babe, be reasonable. You can't go traipsing around abandoned ghost towns, off the beaten track, all by yourself. It isn't safe. I won't allow it."

Safe. He wouldn't allow it. Both comments unsettled her. She was a grown woman. She wouldn't be told what she'd be allowed to do. And suddenly "safe" had lost some of its appeal.

"I'm going," she insisted.

"Why can't you just wait until the franchise deal is settled? Then we'll go. I promise, babe."

"That's what you said before. You broke our date last night—only the latest example of how much your business runs your life. There will just be some new business problem that needs your attention. I'm going, Paul." She was trying to pretend Zack wasn't in the room. Trying to pretend she wasn't taking a strong stand because he was.

Paul looked over at Zack and groaned. "I wish I could be a scoundrel with the ladies like you, old buddy. This love business is damned inconvenient."

Zack's only answer was an amused grin.

"But that's it!" Paul snapped his fingers in sudden inspiration. "You can go with Victoria. You're at liberty for a week, since you won't have to run Desperado's for me. I'd sure feel a lot better if I knew you were looking after Victoria."

"No!" Victoria shouted, then blushed with bright color at her outburst, as both men turned to look at her.

"Why not?" Paul asked, truly surprised at her refusal.

"Yes—why not?" Zack dared her.

Oh my god, he's going to make this difficult! Fumbling for an answer, she finally said, "Because...because I'm, ah..."

Zack let her twist in the wind a moment, then said, "Afraid?"

Victoria glared at him, then turned to Paul. "I want to go with you, not— This is impossible."

"Why?" Paul was getting a little embarrassed in front of his friend. It wasn't like Victoria to be so rude. And yet Zack seemed to be enjoying her obstinacy, probably because it was a change for him from the usual quick acquiesence of beautiful women to his wishes.

"Paul, I can't go on vacation with...*him!* He's a t-total stranger," she stammered, thinking she'd put an end to the embarrassing situation.

"Babe, for Pete's sake! Zack is my best friend. I trust him." Paul's exasperation that she'd even brought it up astonished her. She was stunned to find Paul took her for granted...completely.

She had no intention of going anywhere with Zack. Pretending agreement, but planning to get an early morning start before anyone could join her, she murmured, "Fine...I'll go with your trustworthy friend here." Her tone of voice escaped Paul's notice, and only Victoria saw the speculative glint in Zack's dark eyes as he smiled victoriously.

"Great, then it's agreed?" Paul sighed, looking over at Zack, who nodded his assent.

Victoria's nervousness caused her to sneeze suddenly several times, and she accepted Zack's proffered handkerchief. She held it to her nose, inhaling the warm scent of him, the clean starchy feel of it transporting her....

The featherbed was soft beneath her slender body, cushioning the weight of the gunslinger, who lay sprawled across her, pinning her to the bed. Her face felt flushed from the exertion of trying to slide from beneath his long, fit body. He was fully clothed, from the top of his weatherbeaten black Stetson right down to his dusty cowboy boots, while she was in shocking dishabille.

Her dark tresses had tumbled loose in the struggle and now fanned out in careless disarray on the snowy pillow beneath her. She was naked under the silk dressing gown and watched in what seemed like slow motion as his strong yet gentle hand untied the knotted sash at her waist with ease. Untying ladies' robes one-handed was obviously not new sport for him. He continued to hold her wrists captured above her head on the bed while his free hand opened her robe, baring her to the waist. She felt the cool air slide over her and the peaks of her breasts tightening in response.

And then he did the strangest thing. Instead of looking at what he'd uncovered, he continued to look into her eyes as he cupped her and squeezed gently. Her eyes darkened from pale aqua to a deeper shade of aquamarine in response to his sensual caress.

"Victoria!"

"What?" she answered, shaking her head to clear it as the fantasy slipped away.

Why was Zack staring at her so strangely? She gave him a puzzled look, her eyes the same deep aquamarine they'd been when she'd fled his arms the night before.

Paul's voice was impatient. "I've asked you twice where you'd like to go with Zack and me for lunch. Didn't you sleep at all last night?"

Victoria ignored his question about her sleepless night, ignored Zack, who seemed to be smirking as if he knew he'd been the cause. "You asked me twice...really? Sorry. Guess I just wandered off. Zack is the guest—why don't you let him choose what he wants?"

She immediately wanted to take her words back when Zack stared at her as if she was on the menu. Her face colored, but she refused to look away, and glared at him instead. The man had enough insolence for two sixteen-year-olds.

Finally his eyes shifted to Paul. "Didn't you say something about a brunch at Casa? That sounds good to me." Looking at Victoria accusingly, he added, "I've been hungry for something hot and spicy since last night."

Paul seemed oblivious to the undercurrents of the conversation and left to get the car, grumbling, "Mexican food again."

While they waited for Paul in front of Desperado's, Victoria refused to look at Zack.

This couldn't be happening, she thought. It was like the proverbial snowball, her reckless act last night growing worse with each passing second. And Paul's friend was enjoying every single bit of her discomfort.

At the moment a double homicide seemed very appealing. Killing Paul and Zack would get her a nice quiet place to rest. A cell where she couldn't get into any trouble.

Except in her dreams.

Zack leaned forward and whispered against Victoria's ear. "Satisfy my curiosity...was it me you took along on that little mind trip back there?"

"What?"

His grin was pure sin as he winked and suggested, "I just thought maybe you'd remembered last night and realized what a, um, *satisfying* traveling companion I'm going to make."

"Pl-lease!" Victoria groaned at his conceit, rolling her eyes as she turned her back.

His rich chuckle was somehow familiar.

2

IF VICTORIA WERE to believe the reminiscing Paul and Zack had been doing since brunch, Zack had been a shy, sensitive teenager. It had been Paul who had cut a swath through the eligible ladies of their hometown. It was easy to see that could have been true of Paul. He still had charm enough to spare, even if he didn't choose to use it on the ladies so much anymore, but rather to gain success in business. On the other hand, Zack certainly didn't give any evidence of being sensitive to her feelings. Except for that flash of understanding he'd seemed to show last night in the parking lot of Desperado's, he'd done his best to be rude, crude and socially unacceptable to her.

The years he'd spent in Los Angeles must have changed him. Why? Paul had said the more of a scoundrel with the ladies Zack acted, the better they liked him. He probably spent his spare time beating women off with a stick. Well, he didn't have to worry about her. She was either going to make him a friend or ignore him, and at this point, ignoring him appealed to her because that meant she could ignore all the other feelings he stirred up in her. Feelings that went way beyond friendship. She was more aware of him as a man than a harmless friendship would allow. But ignoring him wasn't going to be easy. And there was no way he'd be traveling with her. She planned to set her alarm and be long gone before the departure time they'd agreed on. She smiled a secret smile of satisfaction as she sipped the sweet, intoxicating drink. Let Paul and Zack take her for granted....

"How about another beer before we call it a night, Paul?" Zack asked, rising from his chair to put in his order at Desperado's bar, crowded now with late-night revelers.

"Sure, but somehow they don't taste as good when I'm buying," Paul bantered, as Zack went to add the drinks to the house tab.

Zack's assertive persistence got the busy bartender's attention quickly, and he was back at their table in minutes. He set a cold bottle of beer in front of Paul and took a swig from his own before setting another strawberry margarita in front of Victoria.

Paul shook his head. "You shouldn't have bought that for Victoria. She never drinks more than one."

Zack eyed the one she'd been nursing all evening. "Surely she can handle more than one of those little kid drinks?" Zack's eyes flashed his dare.

Victoria pushed her empty glass away and pulled the fresh one toward her, biting her tongue to keep from telling him how insufferable he was. Her teeth were already numb, but there was no way she was going to let him insult her womanhood. Although why it was important to her that he think of her as a woman was something she didn't want to dwell on.

The dance floor filled as the band began a slow love song. In minutes all the ladies had been partnered, leaving a scattering of urban cowboys at the bar.

"I think one of us had better dance with Victoria," Zack said.

"I don't want to dance," Victoria said querulously, perturbed by his solicitation.

Zack ignored her and spoke to Paul. "There're at least three cowboys at the bar eyeing Victoria and working up their nerve. Why don't we decide which one of us she gets the way we did in college?"

Paul grinned at his challenge and lifted his beer to his lips. "Ready when you are, pardner."

Victoria watched in amazement as two grown men chugged their bottles of beer, their throats working convulsively. And she was worried about appearing childish!

Paul won. The grin on his face was as wide as a ten-year-old's at a school picnic. Victoria was chagrined at his triumphant, "Beat you." He hadn't said, "I win." She wondered if Zack would have.

Paul seemed to claim her hand as an afterthought, checking a cowboy's advance from the bar. When they reached the edge of the dance floor, he pulled Victoria possessively into his arms. It was a gesture of ownership more than one of passion.

Zack watched them drift across the dance floor, wondering if she cared at all for Paul when he saw her smile up at something Paul said. Was she marrying him for his money? Paul was already comfortably off and it was easy to see that one day he'd be a wealthy man. She obviously liked nice things. Her clothing was mostly made of natural fibers, and that was expensive in these days of synthetics. The late-model sports car she drove wasn't inexpensive, either.

Did she have a career that could subsidize the kind of life-style a woman like her wanted? Did she even have a career? Maybe her parents were indulgent now, and later she planned to move on to an indulgent husband who would give her what she wanted, at least materially.

The muscle in the side of his jaw worked as Victoria entered his view again, and he watched the way Paul held her in his arms. The embrace was careless. She wasn't the right sort of woman for Paul. Paul wouldn't know what to do with a wife like Victoria.

He knew Paul better than anyone. Knew that all of his friend's ambition was tied up in his business. That was where Paul's passion lay. If Zack needed proof of that he had to only remember Victoria in his own arms last night.

She'd been hungry, so very hungry....

The song ended, and Paul and Victoria rejoined him at the table.

"I guess I'd best be turning in, since I've got a long

drive ahead of me tomorrow. Do me a favor, pal." Zack winked at Paul. "Keep the good-bye short tonight when you take her home. I want her in condition to travel."

Victoria glared over the top of her drink at Zack's impertinence, jumping in surprise at the slurping noise her straw made, telling her she'd finished her *second* drink without even being aware of it.

Zack laughed at the abashed look on her face. "You'd better get Victoria home while she can still walk," he teased.

Victoria was all huffy indignation. "I'll have you know I'm a fully operational human being. I can walk just fine, thank you. And *I'm* driving tomorrow, not you," she added, forgetting for a moment that the point was moot, as she planned to leave before he got to her house. She'd say good-bye to Paul tonight.

Zack took the wind out of her sails by standing and backing up humorously, raising his palms in front of him protectively. "Okay, okay...relax." He looked over at Paul. "You're gonna have your hands full with her temper. Are you sure about this marriage?"

Paul laughed. "Her temper seems to have arrived with you." He reached over and hugged Victoria. "Take good care of her, Zack. I'm counting on you to protect her...though if you don't quit rubbing her the wrong way, I'm afraid you'll be the one who'll need protection. Why don't the two of you declare a truce?"

Zack looked over at Victoria and chuckled softly.

He wouldn't dare.

He did. "Is Paul right, Victoria? Have I been rubbing you the wrong way?" His eyes said, *You could have fooled me,* as he stretched slowly, a sensuous dancer's stretch.

When Victoria didn't pick up his bait, he reached down for his beer and drained the last swallow, then smiled. "Tell you what...to show you I'm not a chauvinist pig about driving, I'll toss you for it tomorrow morning."

As she watched his broad shoulders retreating, she had the distinct impression that what he'd just said didn't have anything to do with a coin....

THE NEXT MORNING the sunlight spilled in through the lacy curtains to form a pattern on the dark navy quilt. Victoria glanced down in puzzlement at the old-fashioned, frilly white chemise she had on. She didn't remember owning anything like it.

A movement at the foot of her bed caught her eye. Why wasn't she surprised to see a man dressed in black standing there? While she stared at him he took off his black Stetson and sailed it through the air to land with authority on the bedpost. Bedpost? She didn't have a four-poster bed. Now that she looked around, it occurred to her that this wasn't her bedroom at all. But that *was* her antique dressing table, wasn't it? There behind the stranger in black, whose hands were reaching to unbuckle the leather gun holster that rode low across his lean hips.

At precisely that moment an insistent pounding commenced at the door and Victoria awoke with a start. *What? Who was making such an ungodly racket at her door this early in the morning?* Her fingers reached to massage her head, which was throbbing achingly. She looked over at the alarm clock. *No! It couldn't possibly be eleven o'clock.* She must have forgotten to set her alarm last night. And that commotion at the front door would no doubt be Paul's friend, her unwelcome companion on her trip, all set to start the drive and expecting her to be ready to leave as well. So much for her plan to leave early without him.

Trying to force open her eyes, Victoria slid out of bed and steadied herself a moment before reaching for her kimono from the closet. The room was tilting only slightly, and if she walked very carefully she could make her way to the front door...maybe. Why couldn't she learn that those pretty strawberry margaritas weren't as innocent as they tasted? Why had Paul let her drink more than one? Ah, she remembered now. Zack had brought it to her over Paul's objections, with some crack about a woman being able to handle more than one drink. She concentrated, trying to remember the rest of the evening.

Vaguely she recalled having a little talk with Paul about his taking her for granted and his promising not to let it happen again. But she couldn't remember saying good-night to him. Had she passed out on him? How dreadfully embarrassing.

And now this, she thought, as the pounding on the front door persisted. She yelled out, "Coming," only to be sorry when the sound reverberated in her aching head. She was still struggling to tie the kimono's sash when she opened her door to Zack.

He took in her tousled curls and her sleepy sensuality as she tried unsuccessfully to generate the motor skills necessary to close her kimono by tying its sash in a bow. His eyes were amused and smiled his appreciation of her appearance and condition as he said, "Well at least the wait was worth it."

Victoria stood there dumbly fumbling with her sash, unable to think of what to say. She was not a morning person and there was nothing worse in her mind than waking up to someone who greeted the morning cheerfully. It was one more thing to add to the list of Zack DeLuca's sins.

He took her by the shoulder and moved her aside so he could come in and close the door. "Could I ask you a question?" he asked wryly.

"Only if you wipe that smile off your face," Victoria answered grumpily.

"Are you trying to tie or untie that sash? Either way I'd be glad to be of assistance. Course, if I have my choice..."

"Go away," Victoria mumbled, her lips forming the words with difficulty.

"Yes, well, that is the plan, but you're supposed to go away with me...remember?"

"Don't wanna. Wanna go back to sleep," she murmured drowsily, heading for the bedroom.

"Whoa there," Zack said, catching up to her. He took the sash from her hands and tied it securely, then sat her down at the kitchen table. "You don't want to go back to bed. We've got a schedule to maintain."

She told him what he could do with his schedule and slumped forward to lay her head on the kitchen table.

He grabbed her shoulders and shook her until she opened her eyes. "What you need is some hot coffee in you. Where do you keep it?"

"Don't."

"Don't what? Don't want any, don't touch you—what?"

"Don't have any."

"Come on. Anyone who wakes up as dopey as you must have coffee in the house. How do you wake yourself up?"

"Soda."

"You're kidding..."

Victoria shook her head...gently.

Zack checked the refrigerator, and sure enough, there was a six-pack of cola inside. He handed her a cold can and watched as she chugged it down.

"Are you at least packed?" he asked.

Victoria nodded her head...again gently.

"Didn't you sleep at all last night? Did saying goodbye to your *beloved* involve proving you are a fully operational human being? Did I just miss Paul?"

Victoria ignored his sarcasm and got up and headed for her bedroom.

"Wait! Where do you think you're going?" Zack shouted.

Victoria winced and clamped her hands over her ears.

Zack hooted with laughter, then commented, his voice full of surprise, "You really are a one-drink woman."

Victoria tried to fix her features in a stern reprimand. "You wanna cheer down and make yourself useful while I take my shower?"

"Useful? Like in wash-your-back useful?" His grin was full of mischief as he moved toward her, his look telling her she'd better run if she didn't want to fall into his clutches.

"Don't flatter yourself, DeLuca. The only thing I want your hands on is my luggage. Do you mind?" she asked haughtily, indicating her bags at the foot of her bed. He noticed it was designer luggage.

"Yes, ma'am," he said mockingly, then lifted the luggage like so much cotton candy.

Victoria finished her shower in record time. She was disconcerted somehow, knowing Zack was waiting for her, and not all that certain that he wouldn't try to wash her back.

She stepped out of the bathroom into her bedroom in just her teddy; she'd forgotten her clothes in her haste to take her shower. She stopped in her tracks when she found Zack going through her closets.

"What," she shouted, all thoughts of modesty abandoning her, then winced and lowered her voice to a fierce whisper, "do you think you're doing?"

Zack turned to look at her. One glance at her burgundy teddy wrapped around her soft curves wiped every thought from his mind save one: *to hell with their schedule.* But he didn't care to tell her why he'd been going through her closets so he headed for the car, calling, "Whenever you're ready," over his shoulder on his way out. What he'd been looking for were signs of Paul. Zack found it odd that there hadn't been any.

Victoria rushed through dressing and ventured not a comment when she saw him behind the wheel. Maybe he didn't let anyone else drive his Mercedes. Or maybe there was only one way he did and that involved "tossing" for it.

They hadn't been on the road long when Victoria realized she'd made a terrible mistake. Well, if she was counting, she'd made two in as many days. What had happened at Desperado's had been bad enough, but she'd been crazy to let Zack come along on this trip. She should have stuck to her guns. There was only one way to salvage the mess she'd made of things. Maybe if she tried really hard, she and Zack would become friends—for Paul's sake, she lied to herself, discounting the sexual tension that was alive and whispering between them in the forced intimacy of the car.

They would reach Kansas City by evening if they kept up their current pace, Victoria decided, trying hard not to think about the night that lay ahead. Turning her head, she studied Zack surreptitiously as he drove. He was watching the road with a closed look on his face. His black hair was longish with a tendency to curl on the ends near his collar, and there was already dark stubble on his lean, square jaw. His nose was straight and angular and his mouth was set in a hard scowl. Her gaze followed the prominent vein that ran down the sinewy muscles of his arm and paused to linger on his hands.

They continued to have the power to disturb her. Dark sprigs of hair were sprinkled across their backs and they had a caressing quality about them, as though he enjoyed the texture of the wheel beneath his grip. His nails were clean, his long, square-tipped fingers strong. She remembered the feel of them trailing along her jaw, and the thought came unbidden that she'd enjoy their tactile exploration of her body.

"Looking for a wedding band?" Zack's deep voice startled her out of her ruminations, the mocking resonance scuttering along her spine.

"Of course not," Victoria answered, embarrassed to be caught studying him.

"Yeah, guess not. Rings and promises don't enter into it with you, do they?"

Victoria just glared at him and scrunched down in her seat, staring straight ahead. His opinion of her was perfectly obvious, so becoming friends wasn't going to be easy. Had she just imagined his tenderness in the parking lot that night?

Zack was enjoying her discomfort. He didn't intend to sit idly by and watch his best friend make the same mistake he had made by marrying a woman like Victoria. Surely once Zack had had Victoria, she wouldn't have the nerve to marry Paul, and if she did, he'd have the leverage to discourage her. And Zack did intend to have her before the trip was over. He only hoped sparing Paul what he'd been through wouldn't cost him their friendship in the bargain, though he knew the risk was very real. He knew from personal experience how infatuation could blind a man to a woman's real personality.

The silence in the car grew to deafening levels. When she could no longer bear it, Victoria pushed in the Play button on the cassette system, hoping he at least had a tolerable taste in music. She saw the flicker of an amused smile skirt his lips a split second before the car was filled with the potent, suggestive lyrics of Alabama. Listening to the sensual words with Zack watching her lazily was as nerve-racking as watching a lighted fuse race along the ground toward a waiting powder keg. Without looking at him, she punched the Stop button on the cassette player.

"Coward," he taunted.

They rode the rest of the way to Kansas City in silence, both alone with their thoughts.

Zack didn't care that Victoria was being made to suffer the punishment for his ex-wife's deeds. After all, she was a woman with the same kind of morals, or more accurately, lack of them. His ex-wife, Jane, hadn't been one for rings and promises, either.

Ah, but his plan was worth the risk. He'd make Victoria pay for everything. Most of all she'd pay for the way she'd made him feel when he'd held her in his arms. She'd made him feel again and it was all a lie.

He looked at the pulse beating steadily at her slender neck as she gazed out the window at the passing scenery. She was still hungry...he could smell it. He knew how to satisfy her hunger. He hadn't once, and it had cost him more than he cared to remember. The lesson had been very painful, but Jane had taught him, and he would save his best friend the pain of learning about Victoria after he married.

"So you're a stuntman," Victoria turned and said, deciding that if they were going to be friends, she'd have to talk to him, draw him out.

"Umm..."

She tried again. "How did you get interested in movies?"

"I was dragged kicking and screaming to dance

class. My mother was a dancer and opened a studio. She made me attend dancing classes along with my three older sisters."

"I take it you learned to like the kicking part?" Victoria said with a faint smile.

"Yes, as a matter of fact I did," he agreed. "Even though I went grudgingly at first, in a short time I grew to realize that the discipline offered a way to learn to control my body in a way that sports rarely allowed." And, of course, he'd loved the atmosphere of the studio, being around all that soft, rounded femininity. He'd reveled in the attention and just plain enjoyed the female companionship. Many times he would watch the girls unawares, enjoying their grace and lilting laughter as they worked out at the barre, dust motes dancing in the sunbeams while he did his stretching exercises on the floor. Stretching exercises he still did before stuntwork.

"Didn't you get called sissy a lot?" Victoria asked, finding it difficult to see him as anything but an arrogant male.

"Yeah, I used to get into a lot of fights, and so did Paul, sticking up for me. But when I decided to make dancing a career, I learned to live with the disparaging remarks that are a dancer's lot." An injury had led him to stuntwork, which didn't require the same grace, but did require the timing and body control.

Still, he supposed there had been a cost to his ego.

Doubts had returned to haunt him when his marriage had broken up in its first year.

He'd married young, soon after arriving in New York to pursue his career. His wife had been a dancer, too, a little older than him and already enjoying success in her career. Six months into their marriage he'd caught her cheating with a choreographer she thought could help her further her career. When Zack threw her out, she'd tried to take his manhood with her, telling him that he had never satisfied her in bed.

Since she'd been more experienced than him, he took her word as truth. He had since been through enough women to know that even if it had been true at the time, it was no longer. Now he was always the one to say goodbye. And he'd have been less than honest if he didn't admit taking pleasure in the fact that his career had soared, while the choreographer's had languished.

Jane hadn't destroyed his manhood, but she had destroyed his love of women. Now he only went to bed with women he didn't like.

Victoria didn't feel Zack's thoughtful glance. She was lost in her own thoughts, trying to sort out her feelings. Her unexpected response to Zack was causing her to examine her feelings for Paul.

She had never lied to Paul. She knew she wasn't madly in love with him, any more than he was madly in love with her, despite his claims to the contrary. They were just easy together and complemented each other. She had a feeling she appealed to him because she wasn't needy, either emotionally or financially. Paul wasn't a very giving person, but the flip side of that was that he wasn't a very demanding person. He'd be satisfied with however much of herself Victoria was willing to share.

While Victoria resented her parents because they had been too preoccupied to give her the affection she'd craved, she was also intelligent enough to know that as so often happens, she was like them in the very ways she hated.

She was compulsive like her father and was shy and undemonstrative like her mother. Paul was all hugs and easy handshakes, and that made up for her reticence. She had even come by her career through her compulsive behavior. Ever since she could remember she'd loved clothes and shopping. She followed the world of fashion compulsively and soon found she was spending an inordinate amount of her resources on her compulsion. She turned it into an asset by starting her own business as a personal shopper. It was immediately successful and she regularly turned away business. Unlike Paul, she wasn't ambitious. She was happy with things the way they were. She didn't want the complications of too much success. She'd seen by her father's example that past a certain point success controlled you.

With Zack, she saw the problem immediately. With very little effort on his part, he could soon become an obsession with her. He wasn't easy and comfortable like Paul. He was dangerous to her emotions. He wouldn't be happy with what she was willing to give; he'd want it all. And when he had it all, then what? He'd leave. That's what men who looked like him did. They weren't caretakers, they were takers, period. Men like him belonged only in her fantasies. Where they could be controlled.

He'd called her a coward. She called it being sensible. She was going to use this week with Zack to face down her desire for him. Despite the risk to her sanity, she wasn't going to run away from it. Maybe then the erotic fantasies that had been haunting her would cease.

She decided the best course of action would be to make him like her. And since he made no secret of his dislike for the kind of woman he thought she was, it would take up the better part of the week to convince him he was wrong. She knew what his ploy was. He thought he could make her angry enough to do something foolish. Well, Zack DeLuca was in for a surprise. No matter how rude and nasty he was to her, she would be so nice and disgustingly sweet to him that his teeth would all rot and fall out. She smiled at the mental image of him with all his straight, white teeth missing as she dozed off to sleep.

"WAKE UP, sleepyhead," Zack said, shaking her shoulder and bringing her awake with a start. She blinked her eyes at the brilliant sunset on the horizon and the buildings sprawled around them. They had arrived in Kansas City.

"I suppose you're hungry," Victoria said, rubbing her eyes sleepily. They hadn't stopped to eat.

"We could get a room now and order in...later." Zack grinned.

She ignored his suggestion pointedly and said, "There's something I want to do first, and it's best done on an empty stomach."

He didn't quit. "Isn't that what I just suggested?"

She continued to ignore his flirtations. "Just head across town. Don't be alarmed if the neighborhood looks a little seedy."

His grin widened. "Are we talking a motel with waterbeds and films?" He was enjoying himself immensely.

Victoria groaned at his adolescent behavior. "Drive," she commanded as she unfolded the map she took from the glove compartment.

He groaned the male oh-no-a-woman-reading-a-map groan. She threw him a look of annoyance and continued reading it.

"Aha! Here it is," she said, locating their destination on the map. "Okay, if we get back on the highway, it looks like maybe a twenty-minute drive from here." He followed her directions until they were in a part of town that was a little run-down around the edges. "This is it. Pull over and park."

She did want to go there! It was what he'd been afraid

of when he'd seen the roller coaster in the distance. Well, *he* wasn't riding it. *Under any circumstances.* Not something proclaimed on the big sign out front to be the Rickety Rocket. It was aptly named, too, he thought, as he got out of the car for a closer look.

"Isn't she a beauty?" Victoria exclaimed, flushed with excitement.

"You've got to be kidding. It looks like a piece of bleached driftwood. It must be a hundred years old at least. You aren't planning to actually ride on it, are you?"

"Yeah. I'm into collecting."

As long as some man was into paying, he thought cynically.

"Not material things," she surprised him by saying. "Except I do have this thing about clothes and... well...cars, but what I really collect passionately are experiences."

"You want to collect passionate experiences, let's find the motel with the waterbeds and films. I'll give you a ri...experience you'll never forget."

"I'll just bet you would," Victoria returned. "Tell you what, smart mouth...I'll offer you a dare." There was a twinkle in her eye he should have known better than to ignore.

"You doubt me?" He feigned being wounded to the quick.

"You ride this roller coaster and I'll let you choose our motel tonight."

She'd backed him into a corner, and she was enjoying every moment of his uneasiness. "Okay, I'll get the tickets," he said, reaching for his wallet.

Her hand stayed his. "No...this is *my* treat."

He stood looking at the old monstrosity while she went off to buy the tickets for them. The little amusement park was deserted. What else? No one in his right mind would ride on that death trap. But he hadn't been in his right mind since he'd laid eyes on her.

He saw her getting into the very first car of the train. Wonderful. He'd be able to see death coming to greet him. She handed the old attendant her tickets and waved for Zack to join her.

When he was settled in the front car beside her, she nodded to the old man that they were ready. The train jerked, then took off. It wandered around the circle and began its slow, chugging rise up the incline. Zack tensed and looked over at Victoria. Her face was lit up with excitement, her light aqua eyes dancing with anticipation.

The train slowed as it neared the top of the incline, teasing him with what lay just ahead. They inched closer and closer and then suddenly they were over the top and descending with maddening speed. The wind rushed by his ears and caught at his breath. The bottom fell out of his stomach. *Oh no...!* and then he was okay again as the train settled into a nice easy ride, until the next climb. He looked over at Victoria. There was a thin sheen of perspiration on her upper lip. Her cheeks were flushed and her eyes had deepened to indigo.

He'd seen that transformation once before, when... Oh. Yes, he could see it now, the sexuality of the ride: the slow buildup, the climb of anticipation, the peak and then the catch-your-breath plummet.

They went over a few lesser dips and then the train began to slow as it pulled near the boarding platform. *Thank God.* Zack was just about to rise and get off the train when it began to pick up speed again. "What the he...?"

Victoria looked over at him, all innocence. "One ride doesn't satisfy me. I bought...several...tickets."

Damn! He'd made it through one ride without his motion sickness embarrassing him. He wasn't sure he'd be that lucky a second time. The big hill loomed ahead. What the heck, he had nothing to lose but his breakfast, he decided. He slid his arm along the back of the car, and when they reached the summit of the hill this time, he planted his lips on her neck and closed his eyes. He didn't know if her racing pulse beneath his lips was due to him or the ride, but he knew it was the most incredible sensation. All thoughts of motion sickness slipped from his mind.

Rise and plummet, rise and plummet...and she could do little more than squirm. This time when the train neared the boarding platform, it stopped. The old man at the controls had looked up and caught Victoria's frantic signal.

Zack opened his eyes. "Why are we stopping?"

"Because it's getting dark and they have to close," Victoria lied.

"Oh." Zack nodded his head in understanding. It wasn't so dark he couldn't see the hickey on the side of her neck. He was pleased to see he'd put his mark on her, but somehow he didn't think she would be, when she saw it. That pleased him even more.

When they were back in the car, Zack looked over at Victoria as he reached to insert the key in the ignition. "You do concede that I won the dare?" he asked.

"Yes," she agreed softly.

"And you'll keep your part of the bargain?"

"I don't cheat," she answered in annoyance.

He raised a dark eyebrow and snorted at her choice of words. "Right," he said, as though someone had just told him the Chicago Cubs were going to win the pennant.

"I remember seeing a sign advertising a Mexican restaurant about a mile back...want to split a pitcher of margaritas with our food?"

"Fine," she answered, thinking what she'd really like to do was split a pitcher of margaritas over his head.

THE RESTAURANT WAS SMALL and family run, so they weren't out of place in their casual traveling clothes. The dark-haired waitress brought them a napkin-covered basket of warm tortilla chips and a dish of salsa. She returned in a few minutes with their pitcher of margaritas and took their order for the mixed platter.

They were crunching away, devouring the chips and hot sauce while studying each other. Apparently, the roller coaster had invigorated him, and she was questioning his initial reluctance to take the ride.

Zack watched Victoria sip her margarita, remembering that she was a one-drink wonder. She seemed keyed up. Maybe the second ride around the roller-coaster track had had an effect on her. Maybe she'd get a little tipsy, which would make his planned seduction easier.

It would be tonight, he had decided.

The waitress came with their platter and two plates. Victoria chose the neater things to eat from the platter, like the little rolled fajitas, while Zack wrapped his lips around a squishy burrito. After that he tackled a taco. She watched, mesmerized, as his tongue slid to the corners of his mouth to catch the dripping sauce. He obviously took pleasure in eating, with little regard for propriety. He wouldn't be all that proper in the bedroom, either, she thought, then reached for her drink to cool the flash of warmth the thought brought to her body.

When the food disappeared, the waitress returned, asking if they'd like to order dessert.

Zack looked at Victoria, who waved her hand indecisively.

"Tell you what...why don't you bring us a sopaipilla with a scoop of ice cream on top and two saucers?" he said to the waitress, who nodded and went to see to the order.

"The man has a sweet tooth," Victoria teased.

"Sweet *and* spicy," he reminded her, hinting at other than food as he watched her from beneath dark lashes. The candle in the middle of the table threw shadows across his face. He looked disreputable and perfectly at home in Rosa's Cantina with his dark eyes and day's growth of beard.

Victoria's oversize top had slid off one shoulder, and all Zack could think about was sinking his teeth in a love bite into the soft, succulent femaleness of it. *Ah, here comes the ice cream now.* He could do with something to cool him off. He mustn't rush things.

Victoria cut the sopaipilla in half and dished it out on the saucers, handing Zack his. The scent of the cinnamon drifted up to tantalize them. The sweet, airy tortilla was warm and melting the ice cream to mix with the honey and spice. The cool ice cream felt good on their pallets after the spicy meal. Zack wolfed his down in three quick bites, then looked greedily at Victoria's portion.

"You got a bigger piece. Share with me," he whispered.

Victoria sighed and started to put some of hers on his plate. "No, feed me," he demanded softly. She looked at him and the quirky grin playing on his face, then smiled her acceptance of his dare. She raised a bite to his lips. He put his warm hand over hers, covering it...and then steadying it as she trembled. Opening his mouth, he closed his lips over the soft delicacy as he slid it from her fork. He shut his eyes and chewed, then looked at her and said, "More."

She withdrew her hand from his and handed him her plate. "I can't handle any *more,*" she said, refusing to join his flirtation.

He shrugged and picked up the check, withdrawing several bills from his wallet and placing them on the table. "Come on, let's get out of here," he said.

He rubbed the palms of his hands down his thighs as they walked to the car in the balmy air. She waited for him to unlock her car door, but he made no move to do so. Instead those nervous palms were suddenly grasping her shoulders and his teeth were nipping the soft, naked shoulder that had been flirtatiously slipping out of her sweater all night. His warm breath on her bare skin sent tremors of desire down the backs of her legs. And then she was wrapped in his arms, so securely she could barely breathe. His lips moved from her shoulder, trailing an erotic path up her neck to her waiting lips.

One kiss. She would allow herself one kiss. She had to know what it would be like. Her hands slid to the back of his head, encouraging the strength of his kiss. Someone was breathing heavily. Was it her, was it him...both of them? She didn't know, didn't care. He leaned her back against the car, arching her toward him as he ground his hips into her and thrust his tongue into the warm recesses of her mouth where honey and cream and spice mingled. "Nectar...nectar from the gods," he whispered.

His voice broke the spell and Victoria realized what she was inviting. "No! No, Zack...this isn't going to happen," she whispered fiercely, tearing her mouth from his, gasping for air.

"Maybe it wouldn't have *before* that kiss..." Zack said hoarsely.

"No, Zack. Listen to me...it is *not* going to happen." Victoria pushed her hands against his chest. "We're going to be friends, for Paul's sake...but that's all."

"Is that right?" Zack growled, glaring at her.

"Yes, that's right," she said defiantly.

Zack reached for her hand and brought it to the pulse at his throat. "Do you feel that? *You* did that to me. Now I can *tell* my body that I don't much like you—that I know what kind of woman you really are. I can tell it that till I'm blue in the face. But every time I touch you—you touch me—you know what happens. We're combustible, you and I." Zack's eyes were blazing as they looked into hers, and he promised, "We'll be lovers or we'll be enemies. But one thing we'll damn well never be is *good friends.*"

He dropped her hand and unlocked the car door for her. When she was in, he slammed the door and stalked around to the driver's side. He peeled away from the curb, laying rubber, and headed into traffic, his face a stone-cold mask.

"Where are we going?" Victoria asked when she could talk without her voice shaking.

"To bed."

"I'm serious, Zack."

"So am I."

She wouldn't talk to him while he was sulking like a little boy. After he drove for a while, his body would cool down and his anger would wear off.

When she saw the motel he pulled into, she realized his body may or may not have cooled down, but his anger hadn't worn off.

"Is this your idea of a joke?" Victoria's tone was sarcastic.

"I get to choose where we stay tonight, remember? I had something more elegant in mind back there, but I've regained my senses now. A night with my best friend's fiancée demands something to remind me just what I'm doing and why."

"W-what?!" Victoria stammered, feeling as if she'd come in halfway through a movie. What was he talking about?

"You're not going to marry Paul," he said, as if reading her thoughts. "I won't have you hurt him. He's my best friend. You're going to sleep with me because you can't help yourself. Believe me, it will be less painful for him to find out you're a cheat before you're married than after."

He got out of the car, taking the keys with him, and walked to the motel office. Victoria sat there watching the neon Vacancy sign blink on and off. The motel looked innocent enough. It was a neutral stone color with garages attached to the units. But it wasn't innocent. The hourly rates advertised spoke of its tawdry purpose. And Paul had trusted this man. For the life of her she couldn't figure out why she wasn't afraid.

Zack returned to the car with a key and a bottle. When they were at their unit, he unlocked the door and came back to the car for their luggage. She sat there watching him struggle with all the bags, not offering to help, thinking, *He's got a nice ass.* What was wrong with her? She didn't talk like that, much less think like that. But she'd been doing it ever since she met Zack.

Nothing was going to happen, of course. She would sleep in her single bed and he would sleep in his. She hadn't meant that he could pick the bed when she'd offered to let him pick the motel.

She got out of the car and headed for their unit. When she was inside she came to an abrupt halt. There was only *one* bed. And Zack was sitting in the middle of it. He looked up at her as he pulled the bottle of Jack Daniel's from the brown paper bag in his hand.

Victoria Stone, you don't have a lick of sense...get out while you can! she thought. And then she watched, wide-eyed, as he laid the bottle aside and began breathing into the paper bag.

"What on earth are you doing?" she asked, dumbfounded.

He lowered the bag and grinned. "You'd hyperventilate, too, if you were a man and had to live up to this room. Look at it, for heaven's sake."

Victoria looked around the room. Everywhere that wasn't covered in red flock, including the ceiling, was mirrored in gold-veined, smoked glass. The rug on the floor was red and cheaply plush. The bed Zack was sitting on was round and covered with a black satin spread. Victoria didn't even want to think about the sheets as she collapsed across the bed in giggles.

"You don't feel passionate?" Zack feigned mock hurt.

"Only about getting some sleep," Victoria said. The margaritas were catching up with her. "Come on, Zack, get up. We're checking out."

"Victoria, you can't be serious. I've driven all the way here, I've ridden on the Rickety Rocket and I've had Mexican food. I'm tired and I need my rest if I'm going to chaperone you properly for Paul."

"Go blow that smoke up someone else's dress. I don't need or want a chaperone. And if I did, you'd be the last person to qualify."

"Why is that, Victoria? Is it because you're afraid of me? Or because you're afraid of yourself? I think it's the latter if you're honest."

Victoria didn't answer. Instead she walked to the

bed and pulled back the covers. Incongruently, the sheets were white cotton, starched and clean.

"Tell you what, Zack. I'm going to offer you something you can't refuse."

His grin was cute and sexy, for him...which meant it was lethal for her. "I was hoping you might."

"Calm down, Romeo, or you'll be breathing into that brown paper bag again. Here's the deal. You and I stay here tonight, but you don't try to live up to the room's decor—you don't try anything."

"You're a real spoilsport, you know that? Where's your sense of adventure and fun?"

Victoria's hand closed around a pillow and drew back with deadly intent.

"Okay, okay, you win." Then she heard him mutter under his breath, "Uncultured dame hasn't even seen *Shōgun* and doesn't have a clue about pillowing."

"What?"

"Nothing," Zack said, pausing significantly. "This doesn't change anything—it's just postponing the inevitable for one more night."

"Zack, the only thing inevitable is the fact that we are going to be friends," Victoria promised.

"Right, real good friends...kissing cousins...."

She threw the pillow.

Damn. He didn't want to like her, but he did. He was very much afraid if he wasn't careful, he was going to love her. Would he never learn? Women like Victoria weren't caretakers. They were takers. Hadn't he learned anything from Jane?

He sighed and opened the suitcase on the bed. Too late he saw that it wasn't his. He heard the click of the bathroom door as Victoria went to take her shower. His gaze fixed on the open suitcase before him. The scent she wore, a soft woodsy fragrance, drifted up from the tangle of pastel lingerie. He picked up a lacy garment and buried his face in it, trying to dampen the pain and longing he felt.

"Zack, would you please hand me my robe?" Victoria called, poking her wet head out of the bathroom door. Zack dropped the frothy pink garment guiltily and groped through her suitcase until he came to a robe. He walked over to the bathroom and handed it to her while she stood modesty behind the door, not realizing he caught a daring glimpse of her in the mirror over the sink. When she traded places with him a few minutes later, he was in need of the cold shower he took. The enticing view of bare skin she'd unwittingly given him kept flashing in his mind.

While he was occupied in the shower, Victoria searched for something to do—something that would take enough time so that Zack would fall asleep waiting, in case he had any leftover sexy ideas. Her nails, that was it—they took forever. She had just removed all the old polish when Zack opened the bathroom door. He came sauntering out with a towel wrapped casually around his waist and his toothbrush stuck in the waistband. His hands were rubbing the sides of his ribs as he stretched lazily. Victoria watched the towel slip lower on his hips and gulped.

"What's that lemony smell?" he asked, wrinkling his nose.

"Must be the polish remover," Victoria answered innocently, trying not to stare at him. For he was indeed something to stare at. The only body she'd ever seen like his had been made of cold marble, and it was impossible to study warm flesh dispassionately, she was discovering.

"Damn!" She looked down disgustedly at the slashes of bright nail polish she'd applied to half her thumb.

"You want to keep the noise down?" Zack teased. "I'm going to try to get some sleep while you stay up and paint—" he looked down in pointed amusement at her thumb "—whatever."

With that he dropped his towel and slid under the covers—so quickly Victoria didn't have a chance to object.

She stared dumbly at the towel laying in a mound on the floor. "Wait a minute, you can't sleep...like that!"

Zack opened one eye and looked over at her. "Like what?"

Her face went beet red and she looked away from him as she said, "You know...like that. Without any clothes...naked." She gestured with her hands.

"Is there something wrong with my body?"

"Ah, um, of course not..." *And he knew it.* That was what was bothering her...tempting her. *He knew it.*

"Then why are you so upset? I promised you I wouldn't touch you...tonight. I always sleep naked, so unless you can give me a good reason not to, I'm going to sleep now."

And then, with an athlete's immodesty over his body, he fell promptly asleep.

Victoria watched him surreptitiously until she was convinced he really was asleep. She tried to paint her nails as best she could with unsteady hands. When she finished it was such a mess she tissued all the polish off and gave up.

Now what? She looked around the room for something else to do. She had no intention of sleeping. Tomorrow night she would make sure they had separate rooms. Her eyes lit on the television at the foot of the bed. She didn't want Zack to wake up, because he was much less of a threat to her sanity naked and asleep than naked and awake, so she got up stealthily and turned on the television, leaving the volume low. It was becoming cool in the room, and she shivered as goose bumps rose on her arms. She slid under the covers, making sure that no part of her body touched Zack's and arranged two pillows behind her neck so she could see the screen.

And then she saw what was on it. *Good grief!* She should have realized what movies would go with this room. She was just about to get up and turn off the television when Zack rolled over in his sleep and threw his arm across her breasts. Terrific, now she was trapped into watching the movie. If she moved, she'd chance waking him, and he didn't need any more ideas than he already had. It didn't do any good to close her eyes because, with Zack's arm slung over her breasts and his breath whispering across her neck as he slept, the visions her mind was conjuring up were giving even the explicit movie a run for its money. "Damn!" she muttered in frustration.

She felt the mattress begin to shake softly and wondered if along with everything else the bed vibrated and she'd managed to accidently switch it on. After a minute she realized it was Zack, laughing. *Laughing!*

"Is something amusing you?" she asked crossly.

"Yeah, you are. If you don't quit squirming around so much, I'll start to believe you're really enjoying that educational movie you're watching."

"I thought you were asleep," Victoria said sullenly, ignoring his comment.

He smiled lazily. "I was...until you hauled me over to your side of the bed."

"Me...haul you over...oh!" Victoria flounced off the bed, flicked off the television and sat in the chair. Zack chuckled and fell back asleep.

The hours till morning crawled by at a turtle's pace as she studied him in his sleep. His dark hair was mussed rakishly and his dark lashes threw shadows on his high cheekbones. His body, most of which was visible, was sculpted of muscle and veined in relief. The white sheets were a jeweler's backdrop, setting off his dark beauty, and the black satin bedspread slipping to the floor told a more accurate story of his sexuality. What was it Paul had said? "A scoundrel with the ladies."

Well, she wasn't getting involved with a scoundrel with the ladies. She was engaged to Paul. And she was going to marry him. In his direction lay safety and sanity. In Zack's direction lay her undoing.

He stirred restlessly in his sleep and kicked off the sheet. Dear God, would this night never end?

Victoria picked up the water pitcher from the nightstand and went to fill it in the bathroom sink. She returned to sit in the only chair in the room—the one next to the bed...and him. *Please let him stay sleeping on his stomach,* she prayed, as she poured a drink of water from the pitcher into a paper cup.

"Promise me!" Zack demanded in his sleep, wrapping his arms around the pillow next to him, startling Victoria and causing her hand to waver. Cool water from the pitcher splashed down the front of her robe, and an eerie sensation overtook her....

She dodged back and forth in the stream as someone splashed water on her from behind her. The two horses drinking at the edge of the creek looked up at the commotion.

"Promise me!" The words were insistent as a man's hands slid around her waist from behind.

She tried to twist free and slipped on a smooth rock embedded in the silt beneath her bare feet. As she began to fall, she grabbed for a low-hanging branch of a huge gnarled tree overreaching the stream. She missed....

He steadied her with strong hands, turning her in his arms. His face was shadowed by his black Stetson, and the glint of sunlight off his gun in the holster that he'd discarded on the bank blinded her for a moment.

Before she knew what had happened, he'd released her and stolen the bright blue ribbon from her hair. He reached to the overhanging branch of the gnarled old tree and tied it there.

"As long as this ribbon remains here on this branch, you belong to me. Say it..." he demanded, waiting.

"I promise," she heard herself say.

He flashed her a hotshot smile as he double knotted the ribbon and pulled it as tight as his considerable strength would allow, then watched in satisfaction as a gentle breeze fluttered the ends.

3

VICTORIA FELT AS IF the sandman had dropped half his gritty wares in her eyes. She glared sleepily across the restaurant table at Zack, who smiled back at her and continued shoveling in a huge breakfast, the very sight of which was making her nauseous this early in the morning. She was spoiling for a fight and he seemed determined not to give her one. *He* was feeling fine; she was the one who'd sat up all night in the chair, watching him sleep.

"How can you eat all that food and maintain your incredible—" She stopped herself when she realized just what she was saying. The man didn't need any more self-confidence. Was she out of her mind?

"Body?" Zack finished for her, his eyes glinting devilishly. "It's one of the fringe benefits of my career. I put in long hours of practice, which burns up most of what I eat. And most of what I eat I eat in the mornings. Unless, of course, I have a beautiful lady tempting me with dinner like I did last night," he said with a wink. "As you know, I've got a sweet tooth for sugar and spice and some things not nice...."

She ignored his reference to the intimate dinner

they'd shared and raised the cola that was her breakfast to her lips.

"Unlike you, I take care of my body. How can you put a can of cola in your body for breakfast?" he asked in disgust.

The thing that aggravated her was that he was right. She hated people who were always right, especially early in the morning. "It helps to wake me up," she said irritably.

"Well, if you hadn't stayed up all night watching those naughty movies..." Zack teased.

"I wasn't watching them, and besides, even *my* fantasies are better than that."

He poked his tongue against the inside of his cheek. "Your fantasies...am I in them?" he drawled softly.

Victoria sputtered and choked on her cola. He'd come too close to the truth for comfort. She had to distract him from that line of thinking. "No, my taste runs more to desperadoes and gunslingers." She smiled smugly.

"What?" he asked in surprise.

"You heard me. Why do you think I have a passion for ghost towns? I was an only child and I used to amuse myself reading books. I read westerns as a child because I could identify with the lone gunslinger."

"You fantasize *you* are a gunslinger?"

Victoria looked at Zack in exasperation. "No, dummy. I've just always felt like he'd be the only kind of man who could understand and satisfy me. How about you? What do you fantasize about?" She was more curious than she wanted to be.

"I don't."

"You don't? Come on, Zack, everybody fantasizes."

He shrugged. "Not me."

"Why not?" she asked curiously.

"I live my fantasies...you should try it. But then I forgot—you don't have the courage."

"It has nothing to do with courage, Zack. Sometimes it takes more courage to leave things in the realm of fantasy where they belong. Where they can be controlled."

"Yes, I can see you're real big on control. I wonder..."

"What do you wonder?"

"Don't you ever wonder what would happen if you relinquished that control you value so highly? What is it you're so afraid of?"

"It's not what I'm afraid of...it's what I know."

"What is it that you know, Victoria?"

"That no man can ever live up to my fantasy."

"Oh." The life faded from Zack's eyes.

He drummed his fingers on the table, then announced suddenly, "I'm going to see about getting a picnic basket to take with us. Meet me when you're ready to go. I'll be at the car." He picked up the check and left a tip on the table, heading for the cashier at the door.

Victoria sat there wondering what she'd said that

had ended their conversation so abruptly. Oh well, she'd have more of his company than she wanted on the drive today. And she was determined she wasn't going to let a moody man spoil her vacation. She'd been looking forward to visiting these ghost towns for months. She hadn't let Paul's business spoil it for her, and she certainly wouldn't let Zack get in the way of her enjoyment.

Once they were on the road, the intimacy of the car forced conversation between them.

"Where's the itinerary Paul insisted on making up for the trip? I wanted to play it by ear, but he always needs a plan. I've been so excited about finally going, I haven't paid much attention to exactly *where* we're going."

"It's in the trunk," Zack answered. "I'll get it out at the next rest stop."

Victoria's eyelids fluttered closed and open as the flat stretch of Kansas continued to unwind before them. It wasn't until they crossed over into Colorado that the scenery gradually began to get interesting. Victoria kept her eyes on the horizon, watching for the mountains. Someone had told her that they almost sneaked up on you, that they were suddenly just there. "Zack, look! Let's turn off at this exit. See the sign? There's a ghost town just a hundred miles from here."

Zack gave the sign a cursory glance. "It's not on the agenda Paul gave me," he said, as tiny drops of rain began to pepper the windshield.

"What? Wait a minute here. This is *my* trip. I don't care what Paul planned. We stop when *I* say we stop. He gave up any say when he chose to stay behind."

"Look, Victoria, I'd love to indulge you, but that hundred miles is probably mostly dirt road, and we'd be in trouble if this innocent rain should suddenly turn into a gully washer." He drove right on past the exit.

"Oh, I suppose you're right." She sighed. The man was making an unpleasant habit of being right. "It's just that I'm eager to see a real ghost town."

"Are you sure it's not a real ghost you're anxious to see? You do realize that all the gunslingers are long gone."

"Ah, but I've got a great imagination."

"Do you?" he asked, looking at her curiously. "Well, as it so happens, Paul had a surprise planned for you. We should reach it in about an hour. Through my business connections in L.A., I heard about a ghost town that's been restored so it can be used as a movie set this summer. Seems Hollywood is big on westerns again. It won't be open to the public until they finish shooting, but after that it'll be turned into a tourist attraction—sort of a ghost-town museum. I made a few phone calls and arranged for you to see it before the film crew sets up next week."

"But I don't want to see a *fake* ghost town," Victoria complained with a groan.

"It's not fake. It's restored. The movie people figured

it would be a good gimmick to do a completely authentic restoration, then make a profit on it."

Victoria stayed awake, watching anxiously for the sign for the next hour, until Zack pulled off the highway and turned down a dirt road. "Where are we going, Zack?"

"To the ghost town I told you about."

"But I didn't see any sign." *What's he up to now?* she wondered.

"Of course you didn't see any sign. It isn't open to the public yet. They don't want anyone poking around until the movie's finished. The whole project is under wraps as much as possible."

"Oh."

As they drove along, Victoria noticed a few wildflowers peeping up beside the dirt road. "Wait a minute," she said, as the rain began in earnest. "This is a dirt road, too. How come you'll travel on this one in the rain and you wouldn't travel on the one back there?"

"Because," Zack explained patiently, "I know what's at the end of this road and I know we're almost there. It's only a twenty-five mile drive off the highway. The other ghost town was a hundred miles from the exit, and who knows what kind of wild-goose chase it might have turned out to be? Lots of these old, so-called ghost towns are nothing more than a few boards still standing from the shacks of a miner's camp."

"You seem to know a lot about the West for a city boy," Victoria said suspiciously.

"Maybe I always wanted to be a gunslinger myself." Zack glanced over at her with a teasing smile.

"Look out!"

He swung his gaze back to the road in time to see a young deer jump into the path of the car. He pulled the wheel with a hard jerk and swerved to avoid hitting the animal. The car skidded off the road.

Zack reached his arm out instinctively to protect Victoria and drew it back instantly, as though he had touched a hot coal, when he came in contact with her breast. They sat silently for a moment, watching the deer bound away to the safety of cover. Finally Zack took a deep breath, as if to compose himself, and looked over at Victoria. "You all right?" he asked.

"Yes, I'm okay..." Her voice cracked and then trailed off in a whisper. Her breast was burning from the fleeting touch of his hand and the intimacy of the car seemed suddenly claustrophobic as they gazed into each other's eyes.

Zack looked away first, turning his attention to the car as the rain began blowing in sheets. He eased his foot down on the gas pedal, but the back wheel just spun noisily. He cursed. He tried again, rocking the car forward and back. He tried several more times.

"We're stuck, aren't we?" Victoria said, thinking that was true in more ways than one.

Zack nodded. "This downpour should let up in a little while. When it does, I think we ought to make a run for it. According to the odometer, we're pretty close to the ghost town and we're not going anywhere until the ground dries out a little. This car is mired."

Turning, he reached in the back seat for the picnic basket he'd put there that morning. They shared a bottle of wine while munching cheese and crackers and watching the rain slide down the windshield. He rummaged around in the picnic basket and came up with a sack of brownies. "By special request," he said.

Victoria grinned. It was hard not to like a man who liked brownies.

Zack watched her eyes drift shut as she finished her brownie. "It's going to be awhile before we go anywhere," he said and angled his body sideways on the seat. "Here, why don't you just lay back against me and take a nap?" At her doubtful look, he added, "I promise, you'll be safer asleep with me than I was last night with you." His teasing mood erased the tension between them.

She gave in to her lethargy and stretched out along the seat, laying her head on his shoulder. His own head was resting against the side window; one hand was draped over the steering wheel and the other rested along the top of the seat. She vaguely felt his hand settle in her hair as the sound of the rain lulled her to sleep.

Zack watched her through lowered lids, feeling hungry and possessive. He smiled when he saw she had crossed her long legs instinctively; her sandal dangling where it had come unlaced.

What was it about her that got through to him, when no woman had since Jane? Maybe it was Victoria's unabashed joy in her own femininity. While he enjoyed the aggressive edge many women seemed to have developed, he didn't see why their softness, their very differentness had to be sacrificed on the altar of feminism. Surely they could coexist. He wanted his equal, but he wanted a *woman*.

His hand moved in her hair, teasing the glossy curls, and the woodsy scent of her perfume drifted up to him. He was having a little trouble breathing, so he twisted the keys in the ignition enough to allow him to crack open the window. A cool breeze blew in and Victoria shifted in her sleep, burrowing closer, her lips near his neck while her hands sought the warmth inside his unbuttoned shirt. *Damn!*

The rain slowed, but Zack had no intention of waking her. He was more uncomfortably comfortable than he had ever been in his life. Her steady, warm breath on his neck was doing—had already done—things to his body that bordered on pain. Sweet, delicious pain.

A sudden gust of wind blew through the window and Victoria murmured something unintelligible in her sleep, then twisted so her hips were aligned with his. The pressure was more than he could bear. He gasped her name hoarsely, bracing himself, his whole body tense, and arching slightly toward her. Another gust blew in rain and the cold drops splashed Victoria's face, waking her.

SHE LIFTED DROWSY LIDS to find herself staring straight into liquid fire. The dark pools of desire that were Zack's eyes made her aware of her body, its position, and his state of arousal.

Anger flared quickly in her, only to be dampened by the realization that he wasn't touching her, it was she who was doing all the touching. A hot blush suffused her face as she withdrew her hand from his chest and moved to the far side of the car. She didn't look at him as he drawled, "I hope it was a lovely fantasy."

"It's stopped raining," she said inanely.

"Yes." He moved to stretch the kinks out of his lean frame. "It's time to make a run for it."

He pocketed the keys and came around to help her out, his feet sliding in the slippery grass. "We'll leave the luggage for now. I'll come back for it later when we get our bearings," he said. He did, however, grab the unopened bottle of Jack Daniel's from last night. "For warmth," he explained.

When they reached the top of the slight incline, the rain began again, showering them with cold pellets. In the valley below lay a huddle of buildings barely visible through the foggy mist. Zack's large hand closed around Victoria's as they barreled down the hill toward it. He felt her lose her footing and caught her up in his arms, saving her from a tumble. Rivulets of water coursed down the dirt street in front of the row of gray, weatherbeaten buildings. Zack's boots echoed as they hit the wooden walkway fronting what, if the swinging doors were any indication, was the saloon. The lettering on the sign was indecipherable through the rain. They stood under the shelter of the roof that rested on four timbers and jutted out from the saloon over the wooden walkway. Zack rested his hips against the hitching post as he leaned back and studied Victoria. Like him, she was drenched to the skin and breathing roughly from the exertion of their pell-mell run down the hill in the downpour.

Her tank top was plastered against her breasts and the cold rain had made her nipples stand out in relief. *No...better not to look there.* His eyes moved down to her long, curvaceous legs and wet khaki shorts. *Worse!*

She studied him, too, noting the way his T-shirt lovingly molded the lean indentation along his ribs and clung to his muscular chest. Drops of rain sparkled in his dark hair, then slid down his jaw to his neck. He wiped his mouth with the back of his hand, and Victoria felt his lips with her body. When they were breathing normally again, he noticed her goose bumps and suggested it would be warmer inside the saloon.

As Victoria walked through the swinging wooden doors, she had a sense of stepping back in time and a shiver ran down her spine. She had the oddest sensation that someone was watching her...waiting for her.

Get hold of yourself. Clamp down on it or they'll be carting you off in a straightjacket.

The huge cherry-wood bar overpowered everything else in the room. It stood there gleaming as if it were dressed up and waiting for the night to begin. Victoria could picture how it must have looked, lined with cowboys and dance-hall girls. A chandelier hung from the pressed-tin ceiling over the gambling table and a honky-tonk piano sat in one corner. Flamboyant, flocked gold wallpaper covered the walls, and a gold-trimmed mirror ran along the length of the wall behind the bar. The stairs at the side of the room had fancy curved banisters. All this she saw in shadow, the gray day lending the saloon an eerie feeling, as though it had been slumbering...waiting in time for her. *A straightjacket.*

Zack broke into her thoughts. "Would you look at this place?" He let out a long, slow whistle. "Why this is just like one big playground for you and your fantasies."

He looked at her smugly, his eyes saying he'd take part in any game she wanted.

"Where do those stairs along the wall lead, do you think?" she asked, pointing them out.

He glanced at the staircase, then back at her. "To your fantasies, no doubt. My guess would be this was a first-rate saloon...with rooms available by the hour."

She'd had to ask, she thought with chagrin.

Zack lit the brass candelabra sitting on the bar. "Wait

here, maybe I can find something upstairs to dry off with. I'll be back down in a minute to make a fire."

Victoria nodded in agreement and watched Zack climb the stairs with the candelabra held high. When she heard him moving around upstairs, she wandered back outside to have a look around. She set out exploring, walking along the boardwalk protected from the pouring rain by the overhanging porch roofs. Peering in one window, she caught a glimpse of red-velvet-upholstered barber chairs with ornate wooden arms. Three of the walls were covered with a red flocked wallpaper similar to that in the saloon, and there was an iron woodstove against one wall. A wooden cabinet with a marble top ran along the wall behind the barber chairs and held old tins and leather strops alongside straight razors. Victoria felt that odd tingling feeling again....

The gunslinger sprawled in the barber's chair, his leather boots crossed carelessly at the ankle, his silver spurs scraping the wooden floor. He was dressed in black, his pants were snug. Her glance flicked to his holster hanging on a peg on the wall. The gun in it looked expensive and gleamed wickedly. Shifting her attention back to him, she noticed the black kerchief tied at his neck. She couldn't see his face; he'd tilted his black Stetson over his eyes, as if he was catching forty winks while he waited for a haircut and a hot, steamy shave he badly needed....

"SEE ANYONE YOU KNOW?" Zack asked, coming up behind her.

"No, he's a stranger...." Realizing what she'd just said, she cleared her throat. "No, of course not."

"You didn't see some dude all dressed in black?"

"What?"

"You know, like that guy in the poster on the wall back at the saloon. He looked like he'd be right up your..." he paused and smirked for effect "...dark alley."

She didn't remember seeing any poster. What on earth was he talking about? Was he teasing her? She rubbed the goose bumps that had popped up along her upper arms when she'd thought—hoped?—Zack had seen the man in the barber chair as well. "About that fire?" she said, trying to hide her confusion.

"Right. I was just going out to look for some dry wood. Why don't you go back in the saloon? It's warmer in there and less damp, and I'll see what I can scare up," he said, heading off in the direction of the livery.

She took his advice after glancing back into the now-empty barbershop. When she entered the saloon she saw that Zack had left the candelabra sitting on the gambling table. In its bright glow she saw the poster on the wall that Zack must have been talking about. It was a copy of an old Wanted poster with a grainy photograph of a dangerous-looking man, from what she could make out.

Her gaze dropped to the print below the photograph.

WANTED
JOHNNY BOLERO
For murder in cold blood
Reward: $500.00

VICTORIA HEARD a footstep outside and shivered when a breeze behind her lifted the wispy strands of hair that had fallen from her topknot to rest on her nape. She spun around to see Zack push through the swinging doors at the entrance to the saloon, his arm full of dismembered wooden packing crates.

"I'll soon have you all nice and hot..." he paused, then dared to add, "Or if you'd rather, I could build a fire."

"Stick to rubbing sticks together," Victoria said, annoyed by his constant baiting.

"Woman, you're beginning to try my patience," he warned.

"Give it up, Zack, I have no intention of trying *anything* of yours."

He dropped the wood by the fireplace and came back, grasping her roughly by the shoulders. "I can have you anytime I want," he promised, his lips close to hers, and suddenly it was there between them again—that terrible, fierce chemistry. She closed her eyes, but was surprised when he released her and walked to the fireplace.

"It wouldn't be rape," she acknowledged reluctantly, "but you aren't a man to settle for my body alone."

"Still dead set on marrying a man you don't love?"

"I never said I didn't love Paul."

"You don't have to. Your body says it for you every time I touch you." He looked into her eyes as he struck a match. "When we kiss..." He tossed the match into the fireplace and the packing material caught fire in a blaze. He stood then and placed his hands on her neck, running his thumbs slowly up and down her throat while his dark eyes challenged her. His voice was low and hypnotic as he drawled, "Listen to your body...it *wants* me."

She felt herself lean into him, pulled by the sexual attraction between them. "It wants chocolate, too. It wants a lot of things that aren't good for it," she said, forcing herself to pull away.

"Oh, I'd be good," he said with the confidence of a heartbreaker. The confidence of a man who knew he could please a woman in all the secret ways she could ever want. If he wanted, if he chose to. Leaning against the fireplace he swept her body with his gaze, taking a slow, burning inventory before adding, "I'll just wait, until you get a craving...." He was so sure she would succumb to the chemistry between them that he wasn't even considering failure.

"You forget you're the one who lives out fantasies, Zack, not me," she whispered, backing away unconsciously to put a safe distance between them.

"Maybe you're included in mine."

"Zack, no...I'm marrying Paul."

"Are you? I think not."

He picked up some clothing and offered it to her. "We'd better get you into something dry. Try this. I found it in a trunk upstairs."

Victoria knew this was the worst possible time for her to be taking off her clothes. Zack was obviously feeling playful, which meant he must be part seal, she thought. He didn't seem to mind at all that he was soaking wet, while she was as uncomfortable as a bear with a thorn in its paw.

"Turn your back," Victoria commanded, taking the dress he offered her. She kept her back to the fireplace, not trusting him to keep his eyes averted, but when she had peeled off her wet clothes, she couldn't resist turning toward the fire. Rubbing her hands over her bare skin, she dried herself by the heat of the fire before slipping into the red satin dress Zack had given her. She was having trouble with the buttons when suddenly it dawned on her that the room was too quiet. Why wasn't he giving her any lip? Why had he agreed so amiably to turn his back and face the bar? *The bar!* She whirled around and met his eyes in the mirror. Damn him! He'd been enjoying the view the whole time. If she'd had any doubt about it, his lazy smile erased it.

"Enjoying yourself?" she asked sarcastically.

"Immensely," he replied, unrepentant. "I rather fancy you *almost* in red satin," he said, as she gave up on the buttons and tugged furiously at the low-cut neckline of the red dress. She felt as if she was flaunting her body in ways she never would have normally. It didn't matter that she was wearing nothing beneath it, because nothing would have fit. The satin was like a second skin. But at least it was dry. She tried the buttons again and finally gave in to the inevitable and asked for Zack's assistance. "Do you think you could do something besides stand there and aggravate me?" she demanded.

He moved behind her and she steeled herself not to jump when she felt his warm hands on her bare back. He began easing the buttons open.

"Zack!" She pulled away from his hands.

He reached for her. "Take it easy. Nothing to get excited about. You have the material twisted," he explained with a chuckle. She heard him break off an errant thread and felt him rearrange the material. She held her breath as he buttoned the back of her dress.

"Fair warning," he announced, coming from behind her to pick up the pair of black pants he'd brought down with the red dress.

"Fair warning?" she repeated, not understanding.

"I'm taking off my pants to change. I don't care if

you watch, but I'm giving you fair warning, in case you want to turn your back like some spinster lady."

"Oh!" He made her furious with his mockery. But she turned her back nonetheless.

He chuckled again. "You're not fooling me. I remember you peeking last night."

"Peeking! I'd have to walk around with my eyes closed all the time if I wanted to avoid seeing you without your clothes. You shed them as naturally as a snake sheds its skin."

She heard him pulling off his pants and discarding them. She heard him pulling on dry ones. It was erotic. As the silence lengthened, she assumed he was waiting for her to ask permission to turn around so he could make fun of her primness. Well, she wouldn't give him that satisfaction.

She turned.

And gulped.

His chest was bare and his pants—they were the gunslinger's black pants—weren't completely buttoned. They were a tad snug.

He smiled at her.

"Sorry, I thought you were finished," she said, but she didn't turn back around.

"You owe me a favor," he said, his expression deadpan.

"What?"

"I buttoned you—"

"Forget it, DeLuca."

"Really. I need your help," His tongue was firmly embedded in his cheek. "Men were, um, much smaller back then."

Victoria ignored his plea for help. "The only thing you need help with closing is your mouth, mister."

His dark eyes were full of deviltry as he reached for his fly. Pulling in his flat belly until it was concave, slowly—excruciatingly slowly—he buttoned his pants. When he had only the top button to do, Victoria had the last word, or so she thought. "There now. That wasn't so hard, was it?"

Zack lifted his shirt off the chair and motioned for her to sit down. "Come here by the fire and I'll dry your hair for you. You don't want to catch a cold and ruin the rest of your trip."

She studied his boots, standing to dry by the fireplace. She didn't want to let Zack touch her hair, even though she knew he was right and she would feel better if her hair was dry. She sat down in the chair he'd indicated and leaned her head back, closer to the blazing fire. He knelt behind her and began fluffing her hair with his shirt. She inhaled the damp male scent of him and her eyes grew heavy as they always did when someone played with her hair.

DRYING VICTORIA'S HAIR brought back soft warm memories of brushing his older sisters' hair when he was a little boy...happy to be in their company. Only this wasn't childhood play, this was adult play. His body told him so as he put down the shirt and buried his hands in her soft dark curls, fanning them out in the firelight.

He massaged her scalp, then spread his attentions to her neck and shoulders, his long, supple fingers relaxing her. Her neck arched back, exposing the delicate line of her slim throat as she stretched, offering it up to his hands. She shuddered when she felt them slide down to her breasts, his thumbs moving over their soft peaks until they were hard again, the way they had been in the cold rain. His lips slid seductively down the column of her throat and he wondered if he dared to place his lips where his hands were.

Victoria decided for him, placing her hands over his and moving them away as she stirred from her sensual lassitude. "No, Zack. This is not how we are going to be friends. Let's do something less...dangerous."

"You really aren't who I thought you were, are you?" Zack sighed. *Now what?* He wanted her more than he wanted Paul's friendship, if it came to that. And he hated himself. But it was too late. He'd started liking her...maybe more than that. Did he want to chance measuring up to her fantasies, when it mattered so much? How did one measure up to the perfection of a fantasy? He no longer lied to himself. He didn't want to save Paul from her. He wanted to take her for himself.

Victoria looked over at the gambling table, and a

deck of cards there caught her eye. "You a gambler?" she asked.

"Are you?" he countered softly.

"I've always had good luck with cards. How about a game of poker?" Victoria suggested.

"Two-handed poker?" Zack asked.

"Okay. We could play gin," she ventured.

"What stakes?" Zack was quick to ask.

"I'm *not* playing strip gin with you, if that's what you have in mind." In this dress if she lost one hand she'd be nude.

Damn! Zack's eyes darted around the room for an idea. "Okay. At the end of the evening whoever has the most points gets to choose the fantasy."

Victoria's eyes glowed. The man was persistent, and clever. "On one condition," she said. She didn't know how good he was and she wasn't crazy. "We remain fully clothed."

"Agreed," Zack said, whispering loud enough for her to hear, when he went to pick up the deck of cards, "just like the first time we danced."

THEY PLAYED FOR HOURS, both of them shuffling expertly as the deal changed hands. The score remained nerve-rackingly close. Victoria found it was much more exciting gambling when you didn't know exactly what you were playing for. She'd spent the time thinking of what fantasy she'd choose to play out to keep her mind off wondering what Zack would choose. As he sat across from her, naked from the waist up, she had to force herself to concentrate. She couldn't let him win. Lord only knew what he'd demand from her, with his twisted mind.

She watched his eyes; they were half-closed under dark, straight lashes. The firelight played shadows high on his cheekbones. She found herself paying an inordinate amount of attention to his hands. Was he cheating?

His hands. She had to stop watching them. Everything they held they caressed, feeling for texture and shape. She glanced at her watch. It was close to ten o'clock. The fire was dying. She looked down at the score; they were tied. "Let's call it a game, okay, Zack? Whoever wins the next hand wins all."

"You lose," Zack said with soft delight when she dealt him the winning hand.

"Me and my mouth," she said. "It always gets me into trouble."

Zack looked at her mouth and reached across the table to rake his fingers gently, suggestively, across her lips.

"Yeah, I could see where a mouth like yours could cause plenty of trouble. It's wreaking havoc right now, and you know it."

Victoria pushed his hand away. "I should have just waited out a few more hands, and I would have been on top."

Zack pushed back his chair and put his bare feet up

on the table. His grin became as daring as the mischief in his eyes. "I have no objection to your being on top...none at all. Let's stretch out in front of the embers and I'll prove it."

"Be serious, Zack," Victoria said, getting up and rubbing the back of her neck with her hand. "I'm getting sleepy, so you'd better tell me what you've won."

"A dance."

"A dance?" She already knew that dancing with Zack would definitely be an experience to add to her collection. Did he know that she longed to dance with him again? Or was he doing this because *he* wanted to do it?

"Yes, a special dance. Remember, I told you we'd plug into our fantasies." He headed for the piano and she looked at him in disappointed puzzlement. Zack playing the piano while she danced hadn't been her fantasy at all.

"I said I wanted a dance...so dance for me while I play." His hands hit the piano, producing a seductive jazzy tune.

She stood there for a moment, annoyed. He wanted her to dance to his tune, but she already was. He already had her aching for him to take her in his arms. Well, if he thought he could embarrass her, he was right, but she wasn't going to let him know it. He might think he could sit still while she danced, but he was wrong.

What with the seductive swaying of her hips and flashes of leg beneath swirling red satin, Victoria was as saucy as any dance-hall girl might have been. She moved in close to shimmy and then stepped back to tease. Tantalizing and tempting, she played the seductress, determined to unnerve him.

She succeeded.

Zack's hands had begun to sweat as his body heat rose, and his fingers slipped off the keys in a discordant note.

Victoria's satisfaction was short-lived as she remembered all at once that he had been a dancer before he'd become a stuntman, and she was mortified by her amateur performance.

"Now for the second part of my fantasy," he whispered with a rasp in his voice.

"Zack, I promised to dance, nothing more. Friends...remember?"

"*Not* friends...remember?" He pulled her to him.

"Zack!"

He released her reluctantly and walked to the corner where the Edison phonograph stood. He put the needle down against the cylinder as he cranked the machine up by hand.

When the music started, he took her in his arms, but she held herself rigidly apart, remembering their first dance.

They twirled around the saloon, their steps gradually growing slower as the chemistry drew them closer and closer. She could feel his naked chest brushing against the top of her breasts, bared by the gown's low cleavage. She was breathing hard, and it wasn't just from dancing. Zack was breathing hard, too, and he was incredibly fit—he had to be.

At last, when they were still in each other's arms, his lips claimed hers. Her emotions raced out of control, as violent as a spring thunderstorm. How could she deny his effect on her? The music ended and he lifted her in his arms.

She was drowning in passion, and if he took one step toward the stairs leading up to the bedrooms she wouldn't—couldn't—object.

"I seem to have swept you off your feet, Miss Stone," Zack said in a slow, syrupy drawl. He hesitated for a glimmer of a moment, then let her body slide slowly down his until the tips of her toes brushed the floor. Balancing her, grounding her, he said, "You'd better go on to bed before you sweep me off mine." With that wry comment he turned and went back to sit in front of the fire.

So he wasn't going to make love to her! The man was insufferably vain. She would never let him know how close he had come. Not wanting to overstay her welcome, and not wanting him to think she wanted to be there, with him, she took her pride and bolted up the stairs.

The first room she came to there was a beautiful four-poster bed, covered with an antique quilt. A candle burned on the marble-topped dressing table. Victoria gasped. This was the bedroom of her dream.

Sitting down in a daze before the vanity mirror, she gazed at her reflection. She felt weird and dislocated.

The red dress did something for her—made her look as wanton as she felt. Her hair was dry now, fluffed wildly about her face. Her eyes were wilder still.

She didn't recognize herself, the woman who wanted nothing more than to go downstairs and beg Zack to make love to her.

What was happening to her?

Was she losing her mind?

Or was she discovering the woman in her who wouldn't go downstairs and beg, but would instead go downstairs and insist that Zack make love to her?

The idea both frightened her and excited her beyond all measure.

Something inside her had been awakened, something that demanded her attention. Her action.

How was she going to sleep?

She couldn't act on the fantasy—could she?

Somehow she had to find a way to calm herself, to wait out these dangerous feelings until they subsided.

In the morning she'd be herself again.

4

VICTORIA DIDN'T KNOW how long she'd been asleep when she heard a faint ringing noise and the sound of heavy footsteps climbing the stairs with slow deliberation. A sudden breeze fluttered the lace curtains at the window and snuffed out the candle she'd left burning on the marble-topped dressing table, plunging the room into total darkness. She felt the impression of someone settling on the end of the bed.

"Zack..." she whispered into the darkness.

She'd fallen asleep stretched out on top of a quilt, still dressed in the red satin dress, as she'd listened to the steady drumming of rain falling on the tin roof. He slipped his hand around her ankle, and the satin rustled in the quiet room as he pulled her down the bed toward him. The skirt of the satin dress slid back against the tops of her thighs as he lifted her leg, bending it at the knee, and placed her foot against his hard chest.

The mat of curling hair there tickled the sensitive sole of her foot as he moved it over his chest. She felt the hard button of his male nipple, and then his hands began to gently knead her heel. The pads of his fingertips felt heavenly sliding over the curve of her arch. Squeezing her foot gently with his hand he brought it to his lips.

Her mouth grew dry, her legs weak as he pressed gentle kisses over the surface of her foot and then took each of her toes into his hot mouth. At the same time, he began to caress her ankle, beginning a slow, sensuous journey up her leg.

Victoria lay in drowsy lassitude, allowing Zack to wrap her in his sensuous spell. She didn't move when his lips left her foot and followed the path his hands had taken, sliding hot, moist kisses up her calves.

She was as relaxed and as wound up as she had ever been. He kissed the inside arch of one foot. She'd never experienced her foot as erotic, but it was, and when he got to the second foot it was twice as erotic because she knew what to expect. He went excruciatingly slowly, causing her to anticipate each stroke and caress until she flinched with expectation every time he moved to touch her. When he was again kissing her knee, he stopped, picked up her foot and licked his curled, pointed tongue from her soft smooth heel to her pink toes in one delicious sweep.

And then, before she could anticipate the action, he drew her sensitized foot lower and rubbed it against the hard bulge straining beneath his pants. The simple action caused her to catch her breath as a throbbing began in her core, building an aching desire.

He turned his attention to her other leg and lifted it

into the air, unbent from her heel to her hip. Wrapping his hand around her knee to keep the leg straight, he tucked her foot beneath his chin and began trailing his fingertips down the back of her thigh. The inside of her thigh was screaming for his touch and yet he denied it, prolonging his exquisite torture. And now she felt his palm against the back of her leg, sliding down in feathery strokes. With each stroke his fingertips ventured tantalizingly close to where she ached to be touched. In the dark she knew no embarrassment, only the overwhelming sensuality of his touch on her feverish body.

She felt bereft when he rose from the bed and lowered her leg, but he eased back down on her other side and began again administering his brand of pleasure to that leg in turn. His hands stroked and teased until she could bear it no longer.

With a whimper she grasped his hand and drew it to the moist warmth between her thighs. He slid off the bed and knelt on the floor between her legs, which lay over the edge of the bed. With the heel of his hand he cupped her, applying gentle pressure as his lips feathered kisses of delight along the inside of her firm, sensitized thighs. Every so often a gentle breeze would float in the window and glide across her body, bringing with it the scent of the still-falling rain. At her slight, shivering response, he moved his hands to just above her dark triangle, where his indulgent fingers moved in a caress that heated her blood and caused a flush that warmed her.

She reached for his head, but he captured her hands and pinned them firmly to the bed at her sides. She wanted...oh, how she *wanted*. Her body tried to tell him what she could not say as it arched toward his lips. But he buried his mouth in the dark hair curling over her pubic bone just maddeningly above where she wanted him. His teeth raked lightly, arousing her to higher anticipation. The slow, gentle motion of her hips became wild thrashing gyrations as she searched for relief from the unbearable tension that screamed for release.

At last his mouth slid lower, to the seat of her passion, and she felt the thrust of his tongue. Pleasure beyond her imagining washed over her as she arched and shuddered. Bright colors of a furious rainbow exploded behind her eyes and she cried out his name, her voice unfamiliar to her. Her hips dropped back down to the bed.

She couldn't seem to open her eyes, hard as she tried. So she lay in the dark, sated, limp and daydreaming fuzzily until she fell back asleep. She wasn't aware when the strong hands holding her to the bed released her.

WHEN NEXT SHE OPENED her eyes, it was morning. She sat up and shivered in the damp breeze fluttering through the window. Gingerly she slowly rose from the bed.

When she sat down in front of the old-fashioned

dressing table which matched the one in her bedroom at home, she looked in the mirror and smiled. Zack wanted her, after all. He'd come to her. Now everything had changed. After the feelings he'd awoken in her last night, how could she marry Paul? She felt guilty.... And happy as she listened to the rain, which had slowed to a steady drizzle, because she knew they wouldn't be getting the car out until the ground was drier.

She smiled at the sight she made in the red satin dress and tangled hair. She was in definite need of repair. Turning, she saw that Zack had brought her suitcase from the car sometime during the morning and had placed it at the foot of her bed.

She went through it and set out a pair of jeans, her favorite aqua sweater, which matched her eyes, and a teddy. Not wanting to see Zack just yet, she was quiet as she ventured out into the hall. There was a bathroom with an old-fashioned tub next door. She was thankful to find it outfitted with a towel and a bar of soap...from Zack, no doubt. When she had filled the tub as high as she dared, she stripped off the red dress and locked the door, though she thought ruefully it was a little late for that. She slipped into the welcoming warm water.

As she soaped her body she thought back over last night. She wondered what Zack would say in the light of morning. Would he regret what they had begun or would it have meant something to him? She couldn't bear it if he didn't feel anything but verification of his earlier opinion of her. She wasn't a cheat, despite what he thought. She would never purposely wear one man's ring and set out to seduce another.

What had happened last night had nothing to do with love. It had been sex, pure and simple. Sometimes lust exploded between a man and a woman in spite of their best efforts to defuse it, which was what had happened last night. And no wonder; they were isolated, attracted, and the atmosphere had added to the temptation. There had been nothing romantic about it and she wouldn't start thinking that way. She was going to marry Paul. She was going to tell him what had happened with Zack. He would have to understand. After all, she was the one who had been reluctant to come on this trip with Zack, and Paul had more or less forced her. Paul was as much to blame as she. He knew his friend was a womanizer. She was just one more notch on Zack DeLuca's bedpost; she wouldn't delude herself about that. It pained her to admit it to herself, but she wouldn't flinch from the truth. There was no use trying to pretty up what she had done.

They hadn't actually made love, though...not in the conventional, technical sense. That was reaching, but maybe she wouldn't have to tell Paul, after all. It wasn't as if they were married. And nothing would come of it; she'd make sure of that. She lifted her leg straight up in the air and lathered it. The tenderness of her muscles reminded her of the massage Zack's hands and mouth had rendered last night. It had been such exquisite pleasure...how was she going to go back to Paul?

She didn't have experience to go by. She was a virgin and there had been only one other man besides Paul that she'd gotten close to. But Zack, in a few days time, had actually *touched* her. His gentle sensuality had surprised and delighted her. Was it any wonder that women liked bad boys? Victoria wondered if it was a common occurrence for men who had the hardest edge to be the gentlest, most expert lovers. Now that she thought of it, she realized she had been the only one pleasured last night. She had been loved with no demand for reciprocation, as though her pleasure was reward enough. Strange...

Still, she would have to make sure there was no repeat. Last night could be called technically an accident, something beyond their control that had just happened. If it happened again, they would both be aware and the issue would have to be dealt with, but there would not be a repeat performance. She wouldn't be controlled by a compulsion for anything or anybody. If marrying Paul was what she wanted, making love with Zack could not happen a second time.

She got out of the tub and dried off, noticing a small bruise on her elbow where Zack had grabbed her when she'd started to fall on the run down the hill to the ghost town. She glanced in the mirror to check the fading mark on her neck, the hickey he'd devilishly given her on the roller-coaster ride. Roller coasters would never be quite as thrilling again.

Returning to her room, she dressed and picked up a brush to do something with her tangled hair. When she got all the tangles out, she plaited it in a French braid. She decided to forego makeup, not wanting to give Zack the impression she was pursuing him. The man was vain enough already. She gave her reflection one long, lingering look, then went downstairs.

Zack was slumped in a chair in front of the fireplace, his forearms resting on his knees, his head down and his back to her. She smelled coffee and saw the coffee-pot hanging over the iron spit in the fireplace. The man was certainly capable, she'd give him that. She glanced at the table where they'd sat playing cards last night. She remembered him giving her a shot from his bottle of Jack Daniel's, saying it would take off the chill. It certainly had. Zack and a shot of Jack Daniel's had started a lethal fire in her.

Then she realized that the bottle he had broken the seal on in order to pour her a shot was empty. Bone-dry.

"Morning," she ventured.

Zack grunted.

"How'd you sleep last night?" She tried again.

"I didn't. Me and Jack Daniel's spent the night communicating, so to speak. You might say I spent the night with a friend." He pushed his chair back from the fireplace and stood, facing her.

He had! His eyes were lowered to half-mast, and from what she could see of them he wasn't focusing too well. His beard had another day's growth on it and he looked more disreputable and more desirable than ever.

"So you spent the *entire* night down here after I went upstairs?" she asked, holding her breath.

"I guess so. I don't remember much of anything. You might ask Jack here."

So he'd been drinking when he'd come upstairs to her. It hadn't mattered that it had been her; he'd just been in need of a woman. But she didn't remember smelling whiskey on his breath.... Then she remembered he hadn't kissed her, hadn't gotten close to her in that way at all. On the other hand, maybe he had gone back downstairs afterwards and gotten drunk, feeling guilty for betraying his best friend. Did Zack really not remember or was he just trying to pretend it hadn't happened, trying to forget it had?

He took another sip of coffee, watching her over the rim of the white mug. "We're in luck. After I checked on the car this morning and brought our suitcases back, I let myself in to the general store. The film company has already stocked provisions there for the start-up of production next week. It's a good thing, too, because until the ground begins to dry out, we're not going anywhere. There isn't any fresh food, but I'm sure you'll find something, if you're hungry. I stacked the packaged food over on the bar. I'm going to bed."

He wandered upstairs, leaving her to fend for and amuse herself. She smiled when she saw he'd brought her cans of cola. He wasn't such a bad sort, after all. The rain had stopped finally and sunlight was struggling to peek through the clouds. As soon as she cleaned up the mess he had made, she was going to take a couple of cans of soda and beer and find a stream to put them in to cool. Maybe she'd even do a little panning for gold.

Victoria walked over to the fireplace, took the coffeepot off the spit and set it on the stone hearth. Noticing his boots sitting there to dry, she slipped into them. No use ruining her own shoes. She picked up the empty Jack Daniel's bottle, removing the evidence of Zack's binge, and collected the wrappers from the chocolate cupcakes he'd obviously had for breakfast. She shook her head. All the calories he consumed certainly didn't show up on his perfectly conditioned body. Which got her to thinking. Given his profession, she wouldn't have thought he'd be much of a drinker. He'd be careful of his body because it was his instrument of work. Yet he had bought the liquor, so he must have thought he was going to want or need it. Why?

She went out the swinging doors of the saloon and into the struggling sunshine. The day was already warm enough that she didn't need to wear anything over her soft wool sweater. Walking was a little awkward in the oversize boots and she swayed from side to side with a six-pack of cans in each hand, equally balanced. If she recalled correctly there was a stream not far from where the car was stuck, which was up and over the hill.

Sure enough, as she hiked over the crest of the hill she spotted a little creek at the bottom. Thinking she'd need a way to anchor the cans, she looked around at the flowering shrubs rooted along the path and broke off a few small branches. When she reached the bank of the stream, she wedged the cans up against a large rock, using what she had gathered.

The scenery around her was breathtaking. Mountain peaks were still dusted with snow and there were bright patches of flowers—yellow snow buttercups and pasqueflowers opening in fragile beauty. As she sat there next to the tall grass, she saw a chipmunk burrow under a stump close by a stand of ponderosa pine. She looked up at the movement of a flickering broad-tailed hummingbird. A gentle breeze blew through the leaves of the branches overreaching the stream, rustling the leaves and something else that caught her eye and her breath in her throat.

There on a low-hanging branch of a gnarled old tree was a streamer of faded blue ribbon....

A shiver ran through her as she reached for the tin pan she'd brought with her and bent down to the stream to fancifully pan for gold. She would *not* look at the ribbon fluttering from the branch to see if it was tied in a double knot—the same knot the gunfighter in her fantasy had tied on the branch.

"Don't be afraid...."

"What?" Victoria jumped up, dropping the pan.

"Now calm down, missy. I didn't mean to frighten you. Just wanted to give you some advice. At the rate you're going, you'll never find anything but water."

"Where did you come from?" Victoria asked, backing away warily from the old gentleman in worn jeans, a flannel shirt and long underwear showing at his throat and forearms. He looked as if he hadn't shaved in a long time, and that the reason for that might be he hadn't bathed in just as long. It was probably making him nervous just being this close to water, Victoria thought, a little hysterically.

"I live in an old miner's shack over yonder when weather permits. Otherwise, I live in town. I'm retired and I like to wander about a bit and do a little panning."

Victoria relaxed her guard slightly, deciding he was just a harmless eccentric being friendly. Probably hadn't talked to anyone in weeks. Besides, Zack was within screaming distance—if he hadn't already passed out in a dead sleep.

The old gentleman crouched down beside her and took the large tin ashtray from her hands. "Like I said, don't be afraid to dig down deep in the streambed. That's where the good stuff is."

Victoria watched him, refusing to think about the tree his gnarled hands reminded her of. "Don't be afraid to shake the pan, either. Gold is heavy. It'll sink to the bottom."

The old-timer picked out the big rocks and tossed them aside, working what was left until he had just a little black sand left. "Now if there's any gold, you'll find it in the black sand. Here, you try it." He handed the tin pan back to her.

Victoria scooped up a panful and began picking out the big rocks and discarding them. She worked the remainder around, letting the lighter material slip over the side. She concentrated, clearing her mind of things she didn't want to think of. It was good, aimless work.

"Look! I've found something. I must have beginner's luck," she shouted with a squeal of excitement.

The old-timer smiled patiently. "Nope, that's just pyrite—fool's gold. Keep looking, though. Sometimes gold is found together with pyrite so you never can be sure."

The old man pulled his own tin plate from beneath his flannel shirt and worked companionably beside her, discarding and sifting. "You sure are a pretty lady. You gonna be in that movin' picture they're fixing to make here?"

"No," Victoria said with a laugh. "Just visiting. Actually, we hadn't planned to stay. You see, my fiancé knows someone connected with the movie and arranged for us to visit the ghost town before filming starts up next week. We got stranded here last night when we slid off the road onto the muddy shoulder, trying to avoid hitting a deer. As soon as the sun dries out the ground a bit, we plan to be on our way."

The old-timer nodded as he listened to her explanation. "Where'd you sleep last night?"

"What?"

"Did you sleep in the hotel?"

"No, in the rooms above the saloon. I haven't even seen the hotel yet. It was pouring yesterday and we just camped out in the first building we hit, which happened to be the saloon."

"Have you seen him yet?"

"Who? I wasn't aware there was anyone else here."

"Well, he's here, but he's not here." The old-timer smiled mysteriously.

"What?" Victoria was beginning to think the man spent way too much time alone.

"Johnny Bolero. Don't you know the legend about him?"

"No. I did see his Wanted Dead or Alive poster on the wall of the saloon...but he's been dead for a long time, hasn't he?"

"To be sure. But I've seen him walking back and forth on that balcony outside his room as though he's waiting and watching for Sara."

"Balcony...outside his room? Which room is that?" Victoria held her breath, already knowing the answer.

"The first one at the top of the stairs."

Victoria slowly swallowed the lump in her throat. *Her* room.

"You don't strike me as the type to believe in ghosts," she teased, trying to make light of her fears.

"Jus' know what I saw, is all," he said with a non-committal shrug.

"How do you know so much about Johnny Bolero?" she asked suspiciously. Maybe the old man was pulling her leg.

"My uncle. He usta live in Pitchfork when it was a boomtown. Taught me how to pan for gold. He knew Johnny Bolero."

"You mentioned something about a legend...tell me about it?" Victoria asked, not sure she wanted to know as she faced the faded ribbon waving in the wind.

"The way my uncle told it, Johnny Bolero was a famous desperado. A gunfighter, till he decided to hang up his pistols and retire. He came here to Pitchfork and opened the saloon. He fell for the local beauty and she for him. She was wild as the wind, hear tell, and her parents couldn't stop her when she insisted on working in Johnny's place. Johnny taught her how to deal cards, and she was good at it. Before long she was teachin' him.

"The day before they's to be married, the sheriff—Ralston, I believe his name was—tried to force hisself on Sara. That was her name, Sara Pritchard. Sara told Johnny, and Sheriff Ralston denied it. He challenged Johnny to a gunfight. Now, Johnny was retired but he knew he couldn't refuse to protect Sara's honor. Not after Ralston claimed it was Sara who tried to seduce *him.*

"Ralston had a man up on the roof of the livery, but Johnny saw him. He shot him and Ralston dead, but Ralston's bullet went wild. Sara was killed instantly.

"Johnny was wild with grief. He about drank up every drop in his saloon, but every day, they say, he went to put fresh flowers on Sara's grave.

"He turned gunfighter again, and it seemed after that his draw grew slower, as if was asking to be killed. And one day, a year later, he was. But people say he never left Pitchfork—never left his saloon. Like I said, I've seen him myself up on that balcony over the saloon, pacing, like he's waiting for her."

"What did he look like?" Victoria asked quietly, wishing the photograph on the Wanted poster hadn't been so grainy.

"Well, he was a devil with the ladies before he hung up his guns the first time, hear tell. He always dressed in black except for his trademark silver spurs. He called them his lucky spurs."

Victoria bent her head to sift the sediment in the tin pan in her hand as she thought about all the old man had told her.

"I can see you got the hang of it pretty good now. You don't need my help any longer. I'm heading into town for supplies. I'll stay there a couple of days. If I don't see you there, if you don't get the car out before I get back, I'll bring some help."

The old-timer shook hands, saying it was a real pleasure meeting such a pretty young thing and to be sure to be careful not to let Johnny Bolero steal her heart.

Victoria watched him go, wondering if he was spinning her a yarn for his own amusement or if he was telling her the truth. He seemed to spend a lot of time in his own company, but then she did that, too.

VICTORIA FOUND the constant panning and sifting of sediment in the creekbed relaxing as she continued to wonder over what had happened last night...and Zack's careless dismissal of it. Had it been Zack in the dark? Had she imagined it? Could it have been Johnny Bolero? No, that was preposterous. She shut her eyes against her confusion.

> Sun dappled the leafy branches and warmed her skin as she listened to the sound of horses clopping down the stream toward her. Bandits, she soon saw. Their leader was dressed completely in black. Was it the same man she'd seen in the barbershop? she wondered, noting the black kerchief pulled up over his nose, hiding his face. His black Stetson was drawn down to shield his eyes. He reached for her and slung her over his saddle in front of him.
>
> The men riding with him laughed. "How we gonna divide her up?" one of them wondered out loud.

"She's not part of the loot. She's mine." He looked around the group, his dark eyes dangerous above the black kerchief. "Anybody got any problem with that?" His question met with silence. "Okay, let's move."

"Hey is this a private party or can anyone join?" Victoria heard the deep voice call from downstream. She blinked her eyes and saw Zack splashing toward her.

"Huh?"

"I noticed you had company."

"You did?" she said in confusion.

"Yeah, but the old-timer seemed to be enjoying your blazing smile so much I hated to interrupt."

"Yeah...right. The old-timer."

"Who'd you think I meant?"

"Just him...I didn't know you'd been watching." He looked refreshed. "You feeling any better?" she asked.

"Yeah, almost human. Why did you let me do that last night?"

"What?" *So he did remember.*

"Drink myself into a stupor, of course. What else? Did I do something else I should know about?"

"No, nothing of any importance." *Not to you, anyway.*

"If you give me my boots, I'll carry you back to the saloon, then you can put your shoes on and we'll explore the ghost town. What do you say?"

She slipped off his boots and handed them to him. He pulled them on, then scooped her up as if she weighed nothing. But his mode of transport was piggyback, and he knew just how arousing that was. He had her and his hands just where he wanted them. The man was an arrogant beast. A handsome, arrogant beast, but a beast nonetheless.

He carried her all the way to the saloon. After picking up the shoes she'd left drying by the fireplace, she went back upstairs to her room to change clothes. The day had become warmer and she wanted to wear shorts. After peeling off her damp jeans, she went to her suitcase, pulled out a pair of white jogging shorts and slipped them on.

When she sat down at the dressing table to run a brush through her hair, she caught a glimpse of something on the pillow of her bed. Was it what she thought it was? She turned...it was. Smiling, she moved across the room and reached down to pick up the bouquet of fresh wildflowers. How sweet of Zack. She smiled. She was on her way down to thank him when she stopped and changed her mind. No, he wouldn't acknowledge last night, so she wouldn't acknowledge the flowers. But it did touch her that he'd picked them for her. He must not have been able to sleep this morning, after all.

When she got downstairs she noticed Zack had shaved. He smelled wonderfully of citrus and spice as he walked along beside her, touring the ghost town. As they stopped to look into various buildings, she noticed all the doors were locked. Only the saloon had been left standing open, as though it had been inviting them in...as though it was where they were supposed to stay.

"Do you want to deposit anything here?" Zack asked, as they stopped in front of the bank. "It would be a first if we broke in to make a deposit. How about it—want to break in and deposit *all* the gold you panned this morning?"

Victoria laughed. "No reason to endanger yourself with such a daring escapade. My sum total of gold for this morning's work is zilch. And if I *had* found any, I'd have been much more likely to deposit here," she said, moving on to the next building. Its sign read The Golden Nugget.

"Still a gambler?" Zack teased, looking into the casino. "I thought maybe I'd broken you of that particular vice last night."

"You only made me more careful. I won't be so easy next time."

"What shall we gamble for tonight?"

"You mean *if* I decide to gamble."

"Perhaps you could come up with a better vice to keep us entertained," he suggested, egging her on.

She ignored his comment as he opened the door to the general store, the padlock of which hung open on the latch. So he'd broken in earlier, had he?

Victoria picked out the items she wanted for dinner and Zack carted her selections back to the saloon. Just as they were about to go inside Victoria remembered the canned drinks. "Zack, I left some beer and soda cooling in the stream where you found me this morning. Would you mind getting them while I start dinner?"

"Sure thing," he answered, handing over the supplies.

Victoria pushed through the swinging wooden doors, surprised at how at home she felt doing it. Now that the sun was shining there wasn't any gloomy atmosphere to give her fanciful thoughts. Nonetheless, when she heard a noise behind her, she glanced over her shoulder nervously. The saloon was empty. She walked over to the bar and set down the supplies from the general store. It was then she saw the tin ashtray she'd panned gold with. Someone else had found a new use for it. There was a slim brown cigarette, still burning, resting in it.

She crushed the butt and threw it into the ashes of the fireplace. And then she got to thinking that Zack didn't smoke, so who had left the cigarette burning in the ashtray? Was Zack an occasional smoker, perhaps? She shrugged and tried not to dwell on it. She found some paper plates and served up tuna, pork and beans and potato chips, which she carried to the table by the fireplace.

She went over to get the deck of cards from the gambling table where she'd returned them. Something compelled her to study the Wanted poster of Johnny Bolero. He was a handsome heartbreaker, very much like Zack.

Imagine...the old-timer really believed Johnny Bolero still haunted this saloon. If she were to believe that, she'd be tempted to believe it had been Johnny last night in the darkness...not Zack. Johnny who'd left the cigarette burning on the bar...

IT WAS TURNING OUT TO BE a warm evening, unlike the night before, when the rain had lent a coolness to the air. When Zack came back with the chilled cans, they decided to eat outside. Out front, they sat on a wooden bench, leaning back against the saloon's log wall.

Zack pointed out a large tree in front of the café across the street. "Think they used that as the hanging tree?" he asked.

"Hanging tree?"

"Yeah, you know...frontier justice."

"Maybe. But from what the old man told me, when it came to justice, gunfights were more popular than hangings."

"Yeah? Must be why Johnny Bolero settled here, him being a famous gunfighter and all."

"It's really rather sad," Victoria mused. "Johnny Bolero couldn't have been much older than you when he died. Apparently, he'd wanted to hang up his guns. He'd fallen in love with a local girl."

"Fool."

"What?"

"Only fools fall in love, as the saying goes, though I

guess everyone's entitled to do it once. But a man oughtn't to be a fool more than once in his life."

"So you've been in love before?"

"I've been married."

"That doesn't necessarily follow."

"It does with me."

"Oh." Victoria paused and then, unable to restrain her curiosity, asked, "What happened?"

Zack stared off into the distance. "I caught her cheating."

"And you left?"

"No. I sent her away."

"Are you still married?"

"You have to be kidding!" he answered incredulously.

Victoria shrugged. "Well...some men can handle it."

"Not and remain men." He was definite about that.

"But I suppose it's all right if a man cheats," Victoria replied caustically.

"I didn't say that."

"But it seems to be the unwritten law. It's okay for a man, but not for a woman."

"The unwritten law, when I got married, was that it wasn't okay for either one of us."

Victoria nodded. "You're still bitter?"

"No...not about that. But I'll never forgive her."

"For cheating on you," Victoria said, and she understood.

"No...for cheating me...."

Puzzled, she said, "I don't understand."

"Let's change the subject," Zack suggested. "How about you?"

"What?"

"Ever been married?"

"No."

"Why not?" he asked, finishing the last of the food on his plate.

"Nobody asked...maybe."

"Yeah, right," he drawled. "I got eyes."

"Okay, so nobody I wanted asked."

"Until Paul," Zack corrected.

"Until Paul," Victoria agreed.

"You're determined to go through with it. Why?"

"I want a child."

"*I* can give you a child."

"Generous, aren't you?"

"No. Selfish."

"Well, at least we agree about something."

"I'd provide for my child...he'd never want for anything."

"I thought you were Paul's best friend," Victoria countered.

"I am. That's why I'm making the offer," he lied.

"Right. I forgot. You want to save your best friend from a cheating wife. Heaven forbid your friend should suffer the torture of a battered ego like the one you suffered when your wife cheated on you." Victoria's voice dripped sarcasm that disguised her hurt.

Zack DeLuca was anything *but* a man with a poor ego. He'd made an amazing recovery from his ruined marriage.

"There have been a few women since I divorced my wife," Zack began, then paused.

Victoria shot him a piercing look. "I'll just bet there were," she muttered. And she hated every one of them. That unbidden thought shocked her.

"Hear me out, okay?" he said, gesturing with his hand. "I don't plan on getting married again. But like you, I'm getting to the age where I want a child. Suppose I had it drawn up legally so I'd support our child and help raise him. You'd have your child and you wouldn't have to marry me to get him. And you wouldn't have to marry a safe man like Paul, either."

"Who says it's going to be a boy?"

Zack took a swig from his can of cold beer and then grinned enthusiastically. "Well, if it wasn't, we'd just have to keep trying, wouldn't we?"

"Forget it, DeLuca." She felt herself blushing and noticed he looked pleased by her reaction.

"Calm down. It doesn't matter to me...boy, girl, whatever."

"But I don't live in Los Angeles."

"You could. We have people and shops...you'd be surprised," he teased.

"You've got all the answers, don't you?"

"Yes, ma'am."

"And just how is this child supposed to be conceived...artificial insemination?"

He stared at her hotly. "Not a chance."

"That's the only way I'd even consider your proposal."

"In that case, I withdraw my offer."

"That's what I thought. It's not a *child* you want so badly." She cornered him. "What exactly *is* it you want, Zack DeLuca?"

He stood and picked up their empty plates and cans. "I guess you win this round. I don't suppose you'd care to play a game of cards to resolve our situation."

"No, I wouldn't. I'm not entirely sure you wouldn't cheat to get what you want."

Zack's smiling eyes were telling.

Victoria followed him inside the saloon. "I'm going to bed early, so I can get a good night's sleep for a change."

Zack's only comment was, "Sleep well."

As Victoria climbed the stairs, she could feel his eyes on her. On the landing at the top, she turned and went into her room. It was still just dusk, but she decided to light the candle before noticing that the candle had burned down completely. There was nothing left to light. But she remembered distinctly that last night the flame had been blown out by the breeze billowing the curtains...didn't she? Had she imagined the whole thing? Zack certainly wasn't giving her any hint that something had happened last night. If that was true, she had a better imagination than she'd previously given herself credit for. Maybe it had all been a dream.

She searched through her dressing table for a fresh candle while she searched through her mind for some answers. She came up with the former only.

After she stripped off her tank top and shorts and slid her bikini underwear to the floor, she fell back across the bed, noticing the moonlight glimmering across her naked body. With a sigh she got up and slid under the covers, relishing the cool sheets against her skin. She was weary emotionally as well as physically, and her eyes drifted closed almost before her head hit the pillow....

She was having trouble focusing on the woman walking up the dirt street, but Victoria recognized Pitchfork. The woman was dressed in a long gown of the late 1800s and she was crying. As she came closer, Victoria watched a man dressed in black step out from the saloon and walk toward the woman. He put his arm around her and was leading her away when another man stepped out from the sheriff's office wearing a badge.

"Move away from her," the sheriff shouted.

The man in black didn't budge.

"Step away from her, I said, or so help me, I'll kill you both...her first." Victoria then saw the man with the badge had a gun leveled at the couple. They were still too far away for her to recognize their faces.

The man in black stepped away from the woman with great reluctance. He faced the man wearing the badge. There was twenty yards between them when the man with the badge said, "Okay, since we both want her, I'm going to holster my gun and we'll have this out. Just you and me. It's not going to be her choice. We'll choose who she gets by who's alive after we draw."

The woman was weeping by the side of the street and Victoria rushed to her side to comfort her....

VICTORIA WOKE FROM her dream with a start. When she had reached the woman's side, the woman had been herself!

The candle on the dressing table flickered, casting shadows around the room as Victoria tried to adjust her vision to the shadowy darkness of the room. The dream had smelled of mildew, of damp and secret places.... Usually, her dreams smelled of warm sunlight and happiness. There was something sinister about this fantasy. What was it she'd been about to find out right before she woke up? And why had the woman in the dream been herself?

At least she knew *this* had been a dream. Had she dreamed Zack coming to her room, too? He continued to act as if he hadn't. The only other alternative she refused to even consider. The old-timer by the stream this morning had suggested Johnny Bolero still roamed his saloon. *Next thing you know I'll be thinking a ghost made love to me,* she thought. And she'd been worried about her *fantasies* getting out of hand. There was only one way to find out if Zack had indeed visited her room: she'd have to seduce him into coming back again.

Her decision made, she tossed and turned a bit longer before drifting back to sleep, a vision of a man dressed in black, a gun slung low on his hip, drifting through her mind like a capricious mist.

5

WHEN VICTORIA ARRIVED downstairs the next morning she was groggy; she'd tossed and turned for most of the night after the fright of her interrupted dream. She could feel her grip on reality slipping.

"Morning," Zack said. Studying her closely, he handed her a cola, apparently resigned to her bad habits.

Victoria noticed the overflowing ashtray. "I didn't know you smoked," she commented, relieved to see the same slim, brown cigarettes she remembered from yesterday.

"I seldom do, but I found an open pack on the bar this morning and gave in to the temptation." His tone of voice reflected his disappointment in his self-control, and Victoria couldn't help but wonder if that was what had happened in her room the night before last. Had he given in to temptation and now regretted it? If only he would say something about it. *She* couldn't. What if it had all been her overactive imagination running riot with erotic imagery?

Her gaze swept over his athletic form. Though he was slouched in a chair with his long legs stretched out in front of him, heels on the floor, he was still fuel for erotic imagery. She didn't have to close her eyes to envision her undoing. She didn't have to look any farther than Zack DeLuca. And he knew it. But he was no longer acting on that knowledge. Something had caused a change in him. It was as though a circuit had been interrupted. She still felt the current between them, but only erratically. Only, she suspected, when he thought she wasn't observing him or when he let his own guard down.

Zack set his coffee on the table, rose and stretched like a cat. "I'm going to hike to the nearest phone. We need to let Paul know where we are. He's bound to be worried when we don't show up at the next scheduled stop or if we don't call."

"Good idea," Victoria agreed, feeling guilty that she hadn't thought of it.

"You stick around here and don't go wandering off. If I get back early, maybe we'll have a picnic."

Victoria nodded, lost in thought, as Zack left through the swinging doors. She felt guilty that she hadn't given much thought to Paul since the trip had begun. Why had she always had this fascination with dark, mysterious men? Even to the point of imagining Johnny Bolero all over the place. She had to get hold of herself or she was going to be a basket case.

She got up, deciding to explore more of the ghost town on her own. After all, that was the whole purpose of this trip. So far, all she'd been exploring were her fantasies of dark, dangerous men. She shook her head and deliberately looked away from the Wanted poster of Johnny Bolero, which she passed on her way out.

Taking her time, she wandered down the boardwalk looking in dusty windows of the general store. At one time there had been a second floor to the building, but all that remained now were a few half-burned timbers.

The inside of the general store was already outfitted with various sundries, which she'd already seen firsthand. Colorful ribbons, ladies' hats and a woman's corset were displayed next to spools of colored thread, all partially visible through the dusty windowpanes. The small shop standing next to the general store had a crude wooden sign over it that simply said Drugs. Inside, odd-shaped bottles of various colors and sizes and old-style advertisements for medicine were scattered about.

Winding her way back up the other side of the street, Victoria stopped at the livery to have a look around. She discovered that it housed a couple of old carriages with wooden wheels and one stagecoach carrying old scarred and battered trunks behind the iron rail on its roof. Scattered packing crates gave evidence that the livery had been the receiving station for all the goods sent ahead by the movie company. She went back outside and walked past the mail depot, heading toward the saloon. As she passed the only brick building in town, the bank, she was seized once again by that feeling—that feeling of watchful waiting.

She went through the swinging doors, shaking off the eerie sensation and looking forward to a bath to get rid of the grime from her tour.

While she was soaking in the old-fashioned tub, her mind wandered. She thought about the buildings she had seen and wondered what it would have been like to live in this town back when Johnny Bolero lived here. What would it have felt like to be Sara Pritchard, with a dark, dangerous gunslinger for a lover?

Her hands were slippery with soap on her body while she thought about it. Today, she'd felt almost as if Johnny Bolero had been showing her his town as she'd wandered the streets. There had been a strange ringing in her ears as she'd walked along. She'd had an eerie feeling that someone was trying to tell her something. But what could Johnny Bolero want her to know? She had the feeling he was pleading a case...but for whom?

Victoria reined in her thoughts abruptly. *Would you listen to what you're thinking?* she demanded of herself. *Victoria Stone, quit it and think of something else. For once in your life be practical.*

She thought of Zack, instead.

She thought of him for quite a long time and still hadn't come up with any answers to her questions about him by the time the bathwater had cooled. Why was he being so nice to her, and why had he suddenly stopped tormenting her? Was it because he was no longer attracted to her? Because he'd already proved he could have her?

No, she could still feel the attraction when he was off guard. What then? Was he ashamed of what he had done? Ashamed that he had taken advantage of his best friend's fiancée?

No, somehow she didn't think he would ever be ashamed of what he chose to do with a woman. He wasn't that kind of man. Besides, he genuinely seemed to like her now. She didn't think he was the type who enjoyed hurting women for the fun of it. And if he'd seen he was mistaken about her, he had probably decided to leave her alone. She must have imagined his being in her room...because it was what she had wanted so badly. Still wanted. In fact, the want was building.

Victoria stood in the tub and reached for a soft towel to dry her body. She walked naked back to her room because there was no one to see her; Zack wouldn't be back till later. He had mentioned a picnic. She'd have to see what she'd packed that she could wear to a picnic. Rummaging through her suitcase, she came up with a sundress. The top was strapless, with an elastic, smocked bodice, and the gauzy skirt fell to midcalf. She slipped into a pair of pale blue panties, slid flat sandals on her feet, then sat down at the dressing table to fix her hair. When a breeze fluttered the lace curtains and slid across her shoulders, she felt almost as if someone was caressing her back.

It was too warm to wear her hair down, so she searched the dressing-table drawers for some pins to put it up, but all the drawers were empty. There weren't any hairpins to be found. It was then she saw the hand-carved wooden jewelry box. She picked it up and searched in all the little drawers and compartments, but it, too, was empty. She was about to replace the jewelry box on the table when a sudden gust of wind blew the door to her room closed with a loud bang. She jumped in surprise and dropped the box on the floor.

When she picked it up, she noticed the bottom was loose.

Oh, no...I've broken it! she thought.

Once she'd examined it more closely, she realized it wasn't broken at all. It had a false bottom that she'd jarred loose to reveal what had to be a secret compartment. Not expecting to find hairpins, but too much of a woman not to be curious, Victoria carefully removed the fake bottom.

Nestled in blue velvet was a gold wedding band and an envelope in lavender parchment. She picked up the envelope and read the name scrawled over it in a feminine hand: *Johnny.* She shouldn't read it, Victoria told herself, even as she was sliding the sheet of stationery from its envelope, reading the few brief lines on the aged paper....

18 June 1881

Johnny,

I love the dressing table. What a wonderful surprise for my engagement present. I can't wait for our wedding. Just think, we'll finally be together forever.

Love,
SARA

A tear slid down Victoria's cheek. She wondered if Sara and Johnny had ever been together. She knew the wedding band had never been placed on Sara's finger, and the letter was worn from frequent handling. Had Johnny laid on the four-poster bed and tortured himself after Sara's death, reading and rereading her note, turning the wedding band he'd bought her over and over in his hand?

Victoria slid the letter back into the envelope and picked up the gold wedding band. Inside was an inscription. She got up and went to the window so she could read it in the sunlight. *Love Forever, JB.* She ran her finger over the words. And as all women do when they have a ring in their hand, she slipped it on her finger. It was a perfect fit.

Victoria returned to the dressing table and sat down. It was strange how having the ring on her finger made her feel connected to the Sara of long ago. The ring made her feel safe and protected. She gazed down at the gold band and remembered she would be wearing Paul's soon. Why did that make her feel more trapped than safe?

She decided to leave the ring on while she did her makeup. She liked to glimpse the flash of gold in the mirror as she moved her hands, applying shadow to her lids to enhance the pale color of her eyes. She added two coats of mascara and a berry-stain gloss to her lips. She left her hair down, as there were no pins with which to sweep it up.

When she finished getting ready, she tried to take off the wedding band and replace it in the box. She couldn't get it over her knuckle. She tried again. The ring simply wouldn't come off. She was distracted by the sound of someone downstairs, playing the piano. The strains of an old-fashioned melody drifted up to her. As she left the room, the playing suddenly stopped.

"Zack, is that you?" she asked hesitantly from the top of the stairs. "Zack?" she called even less confidently as she crept down the stairs.

But there was no one in sight, only an open beer sitting atop the piano. Zack must have left it there last night. She picked it up to dispose of it and realized it was only half-empty and still beaded with condensation. A gold coin lay beside the wet ring on the piano. She glanced at it. The date was 1880.

The beer bottle slid from her fingers and spilled on the floor as she considered the implications. She whirled around, but there was no one in the room with her. No one she could see, anyway. Had Zack come back and stepped out again for a minute?

She put her head in her hands as she sidestepped the puddle of beer. What was happening?

If she hadn't begun having these fantasies before she'd met Zack, she'd swear he was drugging her. She even considered that Paul was in on it. That it was some kind of test.

But that was all craziness.

There had to be a reasonable explanation for what kept happening. Only she couldn't think of one.

She busied herself packing a picnic lunch. It took awhile because her nerves were so jittery. She kept dropping things and jumping at the least little sound. When she had lunch ready, she picked up a deck of cards and sat down to play solitaire, hoping the mindless game would calm her, or at least let some reasonable explanation surface in her consciousness.

Zack had been gone for about four hours and she was beginning to feel creepy staying in the saloon all alone. She decided to go for a walk. She'd seen some pretty yellow flowers at the top of the hill leading away from town, so she headed in that direction for a closer look.

It was a warm day but Victoria was cool and comfortable in her sundress. The air smelled of sunshine and was filled with the sound of bees flitting busily from flower to flower. It was a lazy afternoon, which in the city would have found her beside the closest swimming pool. She walked through the patch of flowers, smelling their sweet scent. Then a little building caught her eye and she moved toward it. As she got closer she saw it was part of the ghost town but of a different order. It was one of the abandoned miner's camps that Zack had mentioned, and it hadn't been restored. There were only a couple of shacks left standing. The weather had all but destroyed them. She ducked inside one. In the darkness she made out a postcard and a newspaper article tacked up on one wall. She was surprised to see they were dated only a year ago. Some hiker must have spent the night here and forgotten them.

Thinking it was time she got back to the saloon, so Zack wouldn't be worried when he returned, she headed back through the patch of flowers. She wasn't paying any attention and stumbled and fell when her foot caught on something hidden in the vegetation. She was shaken but not hurt and looked to see what had caused her to trip. It was a large rock. No... Upon closer inspection, she saw that it was a gravestone.

It had been knocked over and was half-buried after decades of neglect. Victoria reached down and wiped it off to read the chiseled letters. It was as if a cold hand had gripped her neck as she read....

SARA PRITCHARD
Born—March 3, 1862
Died—June 28, 1881
In the 19th Year of her beauty

Victoria shivered. So the old man had been right. Johnny and Sara never had gotten together. A bullet had separated them for all time.

A chill ran down Victoria's spine as a movement caught her eye. She glanced up just in time to see a man dressed in black disappear over the ridge. At least she thought that was what she'd seen. It had happened so fast, she could have imagined it. She decided she had. It was the old-timer's talk of ghosts and Johnny Bolero that had her imagination working overtime.

There was a lone, leafy shade tree on the hill, and Victoria sat down beneath it to cool off before heading back. As she gazed at the wildflowers she wondered if they'd grown from the seeds of flowers that Johnny had placed daily on Sara's grave. Or maybe Johnny had deliberately planted them around the time he'd deliberately slowed his draw, because he'd known he wouldn't be there to continue to pay daily tribute to Sara.... Before Victoria knew it her mind had drifted again...

She was in a simple church and she was walking down the aisle...in a white wedding dress. She was walking and walking without getting anywhere. The aisle seemed to go on forever as she walked toward the man in black waiting for her at the end of the aisle.

Finally she reached his side. But just as a veil concealed her face, a black kerchief concealed his. All she could see were dark eyes that dropped to her hand as he placed a gold wedding band on it....

SOMETHING TICKLED her nose and Victoria woke to find a yellow butterfly flitting away. Looking at her hand, she saw with horror the wedding band on her ring finger, as she wasn't awake enough yet to remember finding it in the jewelry box and putting it on. After a moment it came back to her and she began to relax. It *had* been another dream, after all, she thought. But then she saw the black kerchief on the ground beside her.

She jumped away from it as if it were a snake and hurried down the hill. Surely Zack was back by now, whether he had found a telephone or not. In the distance she could hear the faint sound of a piano playing a hauntingly poignant tune. Not the same song she'd heard when she was upstairs in her room and certainly not the kind of song she'd ever expect to hear Zack play.

Cautiously she looked into the saloon, peering over the swinging door. She breathed a sigh of relief when she saw Zack at the piano.

She waited unobserved for him to finish and then

went in. "I didn't think you had it in you," she commented.

"What—the talent or the feelings?" he asked, turning to face her.

"I thought all your talent was in your feet," she said, half answering his question.

Zack rubbed his hands together, then flexed his fingers sensuously. "I play one thing even better than I play the piano...would you like a demonstration?" His gaze raked her body.

Victoria stepped back from his teasing fingers and ignored his question.

"Why haven't you asked me about Paul?" Zack wondered aloud.

"Paul?"

"Yes, aren't you interested in hearing what he had to say when I called?"

"Did you talk to him?"

"No...I didn't find a phone."

Zack pulled his ankle across his thigh and looked back up at her. "It's not going to work, you know," he said.

"What are you talking about?"

"Marrying Paul," Zack answered. "You should have waited to fall in love before agreeing to marry."

"Maybe I got tired of waiting to fall in love. I've seen a lot worse than Paul, and nothing better."

"Been around a lot, huh?" Zack teased.

"Enough to know that most men are just looking for a mother," Victoria retorted.

Zack rubbed his ankle thoughtfully. "I don't think most men are," he said. "Maybe it's just that you're looking for those guys...and staying the hell away from any man you can't mother. You prefer the kind who aren't too dangerous. Yet it galls you that you can't seem to fight the attraction you feel for a particular type of man, so you handle it by restricting that kind of man to your fantasies."

"I don't know what you're talking about," she retorted.

Zack stared her down.

"What kind of man?" she asked finally.

"Me, for instance. I treat you like the woman you are deep inside. Who told you it was wrong to go for what you want—to trust your feelings?"

"Nobody *told* me. I'm just observant. When you go with your feelings, you usually end up getting trampled."

"A little trampling is better than being dead to the bone, which is what you'll become if you keep tamping down your feelings."

"Those are brave words for a man who goes from woman to woman. A man whose own best friend calls him a scoundrel with the ladies. What's wrong with you, Zack, that you can't hold a woman's interest for more than one night?" she asked smugly. "Or is that as long as she can hold *your* interest? There's a place past lust, DeLuca. It's called love."

"Yes," Zack agreed. "But how would you know, when you won't even allow lust to make an appearance? What is love without lust? Whatever you and Paul had, I suppose. I'll stick with lust, since it's all pleasure and no pain."

"You claim you've been hurt, but I don't believe it. You have to have feelings to be hurt."

Zack let his foot fall to the floor, placed his hands on his knees and leaned toward her, his expression intense. "You want to talk about feelings? You're the kind of woman who wants one type of man, but marries another. Not because she's too smart to marry the man who's more than she can handle, but because she's afraid to marry the man who's more than she can control. Why is that?"

Victoria's back stiffened. "Maybe it's because I spent a lifetime trying to get affection from people who weren't able to give it. Maybe I'm smart enough to know there isn't a future in loving a man who can't love me back."

Zack rose from the piano bench, grabbed her by her upper arms and shook her. "But how do you know he can't until you try? What do you judge by? His looks? The way he walks? Something he says? What? How can you make a snap judgment like that without taking the time to get to know a person?"

Victoria twisted from his embrace. "You want to

know how? I'll tell you how. Men like you are born privileged." She waved him off when he began to object. "No, I don't mean financially. I mean physically. You have a certain effect on women that is wired genetically into their female mind."

Zack didn't look convinced.

"Any man who is reasonably tall, and outrageously handsome in a lean and mean sort of way—with a body that won't quit tossed in for good measure—will make any woman salivate," Victoria pronounced. "And when a woman salivates, she does so with more than her body. She salivates with her mind as well. In other words she gets emotionally involved."

"Ah—" Zack said, but once again Victoria cut off his interruption.

"That's why men like you are dangerous. Not because of the physical harm you could do, but because of the emotional havoc you will surely wreak. Men like you who have always had easy access to women don't develop a nurturing personality. You're always taking, not giving—it's second nature to you. Women need to be nurtured. Men like you don't realize the loving you'd get from nurturing a woman makes sex alone pale by comparison." Victoria ended on a whisper, then turned back to Zack. "You have no idea what it feels like for a woman when a man takes her casually. Maybe times are changing and maybe in the future women will be as casual about sex as men, but it won't change for me and women of my generation. We're already mentally wired." She laughed mirthlessly. "Wired so that what turns us on also endangers us."

"Too bad men don't have such problems," Zack said, then waited for her to blow.

He didn't have to wait long; she exploded in a heartbeat. "Right! Men go for brainless, busty blondes and then wonder why they travel from bed to bed in search of 'something.' You'd call that kind of behavior male attitude. What *I* would call it is *boredom.*"

"Well, brainy women don't usually assert their femininity," Zack responded, his voice rising in defense of his gender. "It's like going through a minefield to get to them. And usually a hell of a lot of trouble for little reward."

"Reward? Is that why you do everything? Didn't you ever do anything just to please someone? I had a boyfriend once who made a tape of my favorite book for me because I was so sick with the flu, I couldn't even focus my eyes to read. What made it even dearer was the fact that he inserted his own suggestive comments at regular intervals on the tape. Flowers, candy, whatever...that would have been easier, but nothing would have been as special. It let me know he was interested in *me* and willing to take the time to do something special just for me."

"You mean he recorded *all* of *Gone With The Wind?*" Zack asked incredulously.

Victoria's eyes opened wide in surprise. "How did you know that's what it was?"

Zack smiled, lifting her chin with his finger. "I know women, and the *Gone With The Wind* type is my favorite."

"And what type is that?" she asked suspiciously.

"They feel soft—" He ran his fingertips over her cheek "—smell wonderful—" he nuzzled his nose at her neck "—and they look delicate...despite the fact that they can last the night...." He embraced her with innuendo. "What do you like about me?" he asked, desire flickering in his dark eyes.

"That's assuming I like something about you..." Victoria pulled back from him.

"Let's assume," Zack murmured, drawing her against him once more.

"Oh no," Victoria retorted, "I'm not giving an edge to a real scoundrel with the ladies."

Zack groaned with frustration. "You can't believe everything Paul says. He's the man with the words."

Victoria's eyes danced. "Then you're *not* a real scoundrel with the ladies?"

"Let's change the subject," Zack said, giving up. "Where were you when I got back? I thought I told you not to wander off."

"I just went for a little walk." Victoria paused to remember, then tackled the subject that had been hovering at the back of her mind. "Do you believe in ghosts, Zack?"

"Why? Did you see one?" There was a flicker of humor in his dark eyes.

"Just answer the question."

Zack rubbed his chin, considering. "Well, I guess you could say I believe anything is possible and the definition of reality is different from one person to the next. Does that answer your question?"

His reply was too philosophical for her. She got down to brass tacks. "Have you ever seen a ghost?" she demanded.

"Nope."

"Never?"

"Never. Why?"

"Does this saloon give you any kind of strange feelings?"

"All the strange feelings I've had lately, I started getting at Desperado's, so I don't think this saloon has anything to do with it. Want me to demonstrate?" He waggled both eyebrows.

"I'm serious, Zack...."

Zack caressed her. "This place really is beginning to get to you, isn't it? What is it—did that old-timer tell you some tall tales? What exactly *did* he tell you, anyway?"

"Just that Johnny—" she nodded to the Wanted poster on the wall "— used to and maybe still does haunt this saloon, waiting for his bride."

Zack took both her hands in his protectively. "That old coot's been out in the woods alone too long is all." He noticed the gold band on her finger. "Where'd you get this?" he asked, trying unsuccessfully to slide the ring from her finger.

"I found it upstairs in a jewelry box. I think it was intended for Sara Pritchard. The initials *JB* are engraved inside."

"Well, take it off. It's bad enough messing with an engaged woman, but a married woman goes against my grain."

"It does?"

"It does. Give up the idea of marrying Paul, Victoria. You know you aren't going to be happy. And if you don't love Paul, you'll wind up cheating on him."

"Maybe Paul won't care," she said smoothly. "How do you know we don't plan to have an *open* marriage?"

"Paul's not that crazy!"

"And what's that supposed to mean?"

"First of all, no man in love with a woman is going to countenance her sleeping with another man. Second, and possibly more important to Paul, he has political ambitions that preclude any such nonsense."

Victoria was so angry with Zack that she found herself arguing a point she didn't believe in. "Nonsense! Perfectly well educated people have open marriages."

"Then thank God I don't have their education. If I found my wife in another man's arms, it would be a closed marriage damn quick. She'd be my ex-wife."

"Is that what happened?" Victoria asked softly.

"I don't want to talk about it," Zack said, leaving her and going to the bar.

"It still hurts?"

"No. It's not that."

Victoria wouldn't leave it alone. "Then why won't you talk about it?"

"Because I'd just prefer to forget I ever made such a stupid mistake, okay?"

"Don't you believe you learn from your mistakes?"

"Why do you think I'm a scoundrel with the ladies?" he said, saluting her with the drink he'd just poured.

"Oh."

"Right. But it's wearing thin. And then you had to come along and remind me of all the things I've been denying myself. You made me begin to hope. Until the next day when I found out I hadn't learned so well from my mistakes and that you were just like my ex-wife."

"No. No I'm not."

He stiffened and his eyes narrowed in accusation. "Just like her."

"What *I* did wasn't deliberate," Victoria said, defending herself.

"That doesn't matter. The consequences are what count and you acted on a feeling you had no right to act on. You belonged to another man."

"I don't *belong* to anyone."

"If you married *me* you would."

"I would?"

"Haven't you read the marriage contract, the part where it says love, honor and obey?"

"They've changed it, Zack. It reads, love, honor and cherish now."

"And you're going to love, honor and cherish Paul by taking me as your lover?" Zack laughed shortly.

"No, I'm going to love, honor and cherish Paul by making you my friend."

"Give up the ghost, Victoria."

"You can't see every marriage as suspect just because you made a bad choice. When you got married you were just a boy. Perhaps you made a boy's choice. As a man you might be wiser."

His eyes met hers. "Are *you* a wiser choice?"

"Me?"

"Yeah. Did you think it was just lust that made me walk the ten feet to you at Desperado's? You may think it was nothing but that, but it was a whole lot more complex for me. It was something in your eyes that drew me. You were asking to be loved. No...you were begging. And you didn't beg anyone else at the bar. I watched you walk your eyes down that bar and it was like when you got to me, you knew. What was it about me that made you start burning like a forest fire?"

Victoria was surprised to find herself volunteering the truth. "You were every gunslinger I'd ever fantasized. You were an outsider at Desperado's. A tough guy in dancer's clothes with everyone around you in cowboy gear, and yet you dared anyone to challenge you. You might as well have had a gunbelt strapped to your hips. But nobody challenged you...nobody was that foolish."

"You did."

Yes, she had. And all this fighting was getting her exactly nowhere, Victoria thought. What she wanted to know was whether she had dreamed up Zack coming to her room and loving her or if it had indeed happened. She couldn't come right out and ask him because if she'd imagined it, she'd be embarrassed beyond recovery. And since that night, despite his ribald teasing, he'd made no serious attempt to seduce her. She came back to the conclusion that there was only way to find out. She was going to have to take the initiative.

SHE STOOD AT THE BAR and poured herself a shot from the nearest bottle, hoping to build her courage. Turning, she looked at him. "You're afraid, aren't you?"

"Afraid?"

"Yes. Afraid of losing. That's why you won't fight for what you want. You didn't even fight for your wife."

"I no longer wanted her. It wasn't a question of fighting for something I wanted," Zack answered.

"And me...you use the excuse of saving Paul from finding out what kind of woman I am, when the reality is you want me for yourself. You won't fight Paul for me though, because you lie to yourself. You can't even let yourself admit you want me for yourself. You'd rather teach me a lesson."

"You flatter yourself," Zack said uneasily, watching her move closer.

"Really?" Victoria stopped in front of him. "Then it doesn't bother you if I do this...and this...." Her hands were busy and his eyes were darkening.

"No," he answered in a strangled voice.

"Since it doesn't bother you, then you won't mind putting something on my sunburn for me," she said daringly.

He looked at her sunburned shoulders above her sundress and muttered, "No." He didn't want to touch her. She'd know if he touched her. He splashed some liquor into a glass and tossed it down in a swallow. "I can handle it," he said. "Hand me the ointment."

Defiantly staring into her pale eyes, Zack squeezed a squiggle of burn ointment into his palm.

Victoria forced herself not to move in anticipation as he began rubbing his hands together, warming the cream. Starting with the tops of her arms, he slid his hand to her neck.

As if he wanted to make her feel what it was costing him to deny himself, Zack rubbed his thumbs slowly down the slender column of her throat, until he reached her shoulders. He slid the top of the strapless sundress down as he smoothed ointment onto her unburned yet tender breasts with his large hands.

He looked into her eyes, his gaze penetratingly intimate as skin slid sensuously against skin, each lingering caress heightening her arousal. She could see how easy it had been for him to be a scoundrel with the ladies. He had a scoundrel's touch, an all-knowing skill.

"Zack..." she pleaded, not caring that she was giving too much away too easily.

He didn't respond, just kept teasing her with the infinite skill of caresses that grew ever bolder and more possessive.

"Zack..." She repeated her plea, feeling as if she was drugged with passion and desire. He was forcing her body to betray her.

To betray Paul.

She shouldn't have been surprised. Zack had boasted he could do as much.

"Please..." she begged. Begged when she'd promised herself she wouldn't.

"Uh-uh, baby. Not till you break your engagement." Zack twisted her nipple in an exquisite caress. "Besides, I can't put my mouth on you. The ointment..."

"Damn you," she muttered in humiliation as she fled to her room—knowing she'd imagined everything, even that he might have fallen a little in love with her.

Eventually she cried herself to sleep.

6

IT WAS THE SAME DREAM again....

The woman in the old-fashioned dress was walking down the dusty boardwalk of Pitchfork toward the saloon. Again the man dressed in black stepped out from the swinging doors of the saloon and walked toward her, placing his arms around her and leading her away.

Then the other man, the one with the badge, stepped from the sheriff's office. "Move away from her...release her and step away or so help me, I'll kill you both...her first."

Victoria then saw that the man in front of the sheriff's office had a gun aimed at the man in black. They were still too far away for her to see their faces.

The man in black stepped away from the woman reluctantly and faced the other man, who stepped into the street. The woman wept silently. Victoria wanted to go and comfort her, but couldn't seem to move.

Soon both men were facing each other in the

middle of the street, about twenty yards apart. The man with the badge said, "Okay. Now I'm going to holster my gun and we're going to have this out—just you and me. This is not her choice. We'll decide who she gets by who's alive after we draw."

They were going to try to kill each other! Victoria had to move. She found herself running to the woman in the street to beg her to stop them. She reached her only to find out it was herself in the old-fashioned dress.

Confused, she turned and looked at the men in the street...the man wearing the badge was Paul and the man in black was Zack. No! She had to stop them.

"Draw," the man with the badge said, as he lifted his gun from his holster.

"No...stop!" Victoria shouted, running between them. "No, don't do this, please, Zack," she pleaded. Zack's hand did not go to his holster until the bullet from the other man's gun struck her in the back and she started to fall. Zack's gun cleared his holster with lightning speed and the man with the badge fell to the street.

"Nooo!" Victoria wailed, trying to stop herself from falling, but her arms were held at her sides and she was being shaken like a rag doll.

HER EYES FLEW open, to see Zack's concerned face in front of her. "What is it? What's happened?" he demanded.

"Zack...oh Zack! It was horrible. Please, just hold me."

He wrapped her in his arms and held her, gentling her by stroking her hair as he had the first night they'd met. She sobbed on his bare shoulder and he kissed the top of her head, breathing in her scent. The sheet had slipped to her waist and they were crushed, naked together.

Zack was not immune to the sensations her bare flesh and aroused nipples were creating in his body. The longer he held her, the more volatile the situation became—he had to defuse it. He pulled her head back and looked into her frightened eyes. She was pale and shaking. "You're okay. You were just having a nightmare, that's all."

He wiped the tears away with his thumbs and then kissed her damp cheeks. Her arms were still twined around his neck and he couldn't stop himself from tasting her pouty lips. The bottom one was trembling. He had to make it stop, and there was only one way to do it. His mouth met hers in a sweet, gentle kiss that did nothing to soothe their bodies. The chemistry between them was alive and burning for release, but he fought the urge to set it free. He couldn't allow that.

But then Victoria pulled him even closer to plunder his resolve with the sweetest of swords—sinking her pink tongue into his willing mouth. They both lost all reason as the passion leaping between them flared out of control. She was hungry for him and he was a starving man. The duel was short.

"Don't let me stop you now." A disembodied voice came from the shadows.

"Paul!" Victoria cried, and Paul stepped forward.

"I didn't hear your car," Zack said, not moving away from Victoria.

"Obviously."

"When did you get here?"

"I've been here a while," Paul said with an enigmatic smile.

"What do you mean you've been here awhile?" Victoria asked, confused and startled by his sudden appearance. What was going on? And was Zack in on it?

Zack was quick to respond. "He means he's been spying on us."

"That's right. I gave you a head start and then I followed. I was sure of you, Victoria, until I saw how you reacted to Zack. A politician has to have a wife he can be sure of, and when you put up such a fuss about Zack joining you when I suggested it, I decided it could mean only one of two things. Either you really didn't want to go with him, or more likely, Zack was having the same effect on you that he's had on every other woman who's crossed his path. You knew you'd give in to him if the two of you spent enough time alone together. Looks like it didn't take much time at all."

"Why did you wait until now to show yourself?" Zack demanded.

"I wanted to give both of you enough rope to hang yourselves with."

"You...how could you?" Victoria sputtered.

"I think you are the one with the explaining to do," Paul countered, pointedly looking at their embrace and half-naked state. "What the hell is going on here? I thought we were engaged, Victoria. And, Zack, you're supposed to be my friend." Paul's tone indicated that he might just be more angry over Zack's betrayal than Victoria's.

"Are you okay, Victoria?" Zack asked solicitously, ignoring Paul's fury. She nodded and he slid off the bed, wearing only the pair of jeans he had hastily donned. Victoria was still wearing nothing but bikini panties because of the sunburn on her shoulders. Paul's appraisal told her volumes as she pulled up the sheet to cover herself.

"Get dressed," he ordered. "We'll wait downstairs."

From the look Zack gave her, Victoria knew he would have stayed, but she shook her head.

Zack and Paul left the room in strained silence. When she heard them making their way downstairs, she slid out of bed and dressed quickly. She didn't want to give them enough time alone to tear into each other; she didn't want to be responsible for the destruction of a life-long friendship.

WHEN SHE GOT DOWNSTAIRS she saw the men were not going to be able to salvage their relationship. It was there in the tense hostile atmosphere between them.

"I'm surprised at you, Victoria," Paul declared when he saw her. "I warned you he was a scoundrel with the ladies. Are you now just one more in the legion of his fans who think his tongue should be bronzed?" Obviously, the angrier Paul got the cruder he became.

"Leave Victoria out of this, Paul. Any problems you've got, take them up with me. She's perfectly innocent."

"Oh no, it's worse than I thought," Paul scoffed. "You've finally got your knight in shining armor, eh, Victoria? Know why it's so shiny? It's because legions of women have shined it.

"Go ahead, ask him!" Paul ranted on. "He won't deny it. Only one thing, babe. He's not the marrying kind. He's the one-night-stand kind. Zack's soured on marriage. He tried it once and failed. Of course, he was just a boy then...not the experienced lover he is today. Isn't that right, Zack?"

"You're the man with the words, Paul."

"And you're the man who doesn't need them. God, I always hated you for that. All you had to do was stand there and fight women off. The dark, brooding type that women roll over on their backs for. I've loved you like a brother, but it was hard not to hate you for that."

Paul turned his attention to Victoria. "The funny thing is that he never really cared. Not at all after his wife left. Anyone he ever slept with was just another woman—interchangeable and functional. Does that give you some clue as to what kind of number Zack's dear wife must have done on him? She either broke his heart or emasculated him...or both."

Paul wound down from his angry speech, to be met with total silence. He looked down and saw the wedding band on Victoria's hand. His gaze flashed back to Victoria's face. "Hey, wait a minute, am I beating a dead horse here? Did you two get married or something?"

"What?"

"The ring..."

Victoria looked down at her finger. "No, I just found it, tried it on and it got stuck."

"You're telling me that's why you're wearing it and not my engagement ring?"

"Yes."

"Then we're still engaged?"

"Yes."

"Then what did I see upstairs in your bedroom?"

"Nothing. It wasn't what it looked like."

Paul's eyebrows rose skeptically.

"I can explain," Zack interjected. "She had a bad dream and I was only comforting her, that was all."

"And you think I should believe that."

Zack had had enough. The decision he came to surprised him, though he didn't know why it should. He hadn't felt like himself since he'd arrived in Pitchfork.

He kept having the weird feeling he'd been here before, when he knew he hadn't. He kept seeing things out of the corner of his eye. Kept itching to reach for a gun where it would have been slung low on his hip if he'd been a gunfighter in another time in this place.

"Paul, you remember what I told you before we left? I told you you couldn't afford Victoria. If there was the slightest doubt in your mind about trusting her, then your political ambitions could end up in ruins. You can't afford that now, can you? Or are you a bigger risk taker than I think you are?"

Paul responded as if his manhood was being challenged. "I'm as big a risk taker as you are, Zack—any time," he boasted.

"Then what will it be, guns or cards?" Zack asked, and his words echoed eerily, as if they'd been spoken before in some other time, yet in this very place.

"No guns!" Victoria cried out, remembering her repeating nightmare.

"What guns? What are you talking about?" Paul asked, shocked at Zack's words.

Zack shrugged his powerful shoulders. "Just an expression. You want her, I want her. We'll cut the cards for her."

"I don't believe this," Victoria fumed, spinning on her heel and fleeing upstairs, not wanting to witness the men's foolishness.

Concerned, Zack watched her go, but Paul picked

up the cards right away, cutting the deck and placing it on the table between them.

"Let's finish this now," Paul insisted, drawing a card. Suddenly he looked confident. Suddenly he was acting very confident. "Looks like Lady Luck is with me tonight, traitor friend. You can't win every time."

"Why don't you just let it go, man?" Zack reasoned. "You don't love her."

"Like you do. You just want her because she's mine. Because she's a challenge—a new conquest. You bastard."

"You're wrong. I do love her."

"Right. You don't know what love is."

"Look, Paul. I understand your anger. I didn't mean for this to happen." How could he explain that, sure he'd meant to seduce Victoria, but only to prove she was all wrong for Paul. Zack hadn't meant to fall in love with the woman he'd so misjudged.

"But it did happen," Paul insisted. "Draw your card."

"You're both bastards!" Victoria cried as she approached the table once again and tossed Paul's engagement ring down among the cards. It was distraction enough for Zack to produce the ace of hearts without Paul knowing he'd been cheated.

"You lose, friend," Zack said.

"Frigging fate," Paul cursed. "I've always been good at picking up diamonds and you've always been good at picking up hearts." He stared at Victoria. "Take her, she's yours."

"Wait a minute," Victoria protested. "I never agreed to your dumb wager. And exactly how long have you been here, Paul?" Was *he* the man in black she'd seen? "Answer my question. I want you to tell me how long you've been in town."

"Since the day you got stuck in the mud," he replied smugly. "I left the day after you two did, figuring I'd catch up. It was just a stroke of luck you got stuck here. And then once I was here, I remembered you had a thing for gunfighters, so I decided to give you a gunfighter's ghost to play with while I watched to see what would happen."

"So it *was* you!" Victoria said with sudden understanding. "You were the one who left the cigarette burning on the bar and the gold piece—you were the one who played the piano and left the drink setting on it."

Paul nodded.

"You were the one who left wildflowers on my pillow..." she continued.

At Paul's blank look, Victoria glanced over at Zack. He was actually blushing.

"Why?" she asked, returning her attention to Paul.

"I thought you'd enjoy having a gunfighter's ghost lurking around Pitchfork. Then again, maybe my real motive was to distract you from Zack. Did I really have you believing Johnny Bolero was still around?"

"I had my moments."

"Really? You really believed Johnny Bolero was haunting Pitchfork?"

"Of course, she didn't believe any such thing," Zack stated. "There are no such things as ghosts." It was as if he was trying to convince himself.

"Yeah, seeing a ghost is like hearing Zack say he's in love—hard to believe. I don't know, maybe you are *the* woman to spur Zack into proposing marriage, Victoria, though I must say I never thought to see the day again," Paul said. "And speaking of weddings—don't bother to invite me to yours, on the off chance there might actually be one." He stalked out of the saloon.

At the sound of his heels on the verandah, an alarm went off in Victoria's head at the word *spur*. That was it! She'd never been able to place that ringing sound the night when she'd heard footsteps climbing to her room. It had been the sound of spurs. She looked down at Zack's boots as he followed Paul through the swinging door. There were no spurs there—never had been. And Paul never wore boots.

That meant...

The old man had said Johnny Bolero wore silver spurs on his boots at all times—they were his lucky charms.

Outside the saloon she watched as Paul left in silence, and a friendship as well as an engagement came to an end.

Again she had the eerie feeling someone was watching her. She glanced over her shoulder at the balcony of the saloon. Nothing...nobody. But her eye was caught and held by the sign over the door that she'd never noticed before: The Silver Spur Saloon.

That clinched it. But, no! She couldn't be right. She'd imagined that night. There were no such things as ghosts. There had to be some logical explanation for the ringing noise. She'd let her mind run away with her. Surely though, it wasn't what she thought it was. Zack had come to her that first night, hadn't he? That night he had brought out her feelings. If he hadn't come to her, she would be leaving now with Paul. She would be forever safe and unsatisfied. But Zack *had* come to her—hadn't he?

Victoria knew it wasn't smart to have chosen a "scoundrel with the ladies," but when it came right down to it, she really hadn't had much choice at all. Her heart had made the decision for her the first time she'd laid eyes on Zack in Desperado's. Who'd have believed she'd find her destiny leaning against a bar?

AFTER PAUL LEFT, Zack and Victoria went back inside the saloon with everything still unsaid between them.

"Are you sure?" Zack finally asked, turning to Victoria and breaking the silence.

"Yes. I never should have agreed to marry Paul. I know that now. In my heart, I've always known it."

"What does your heart tell you about me? Are you going to agree to marry me?"

"Against my better judgment," she teased.

Zack swung her up into his arms. "Why don't we see what we can do about that judgment of yours?"

"Zack, we need to talk. Don't play games with my mind," she cautioned.

"Your mind? Trust me, playing with your mind does not figure in my immediate plans." He gave her a lascivious look that made his intentions obvious.

"You didn't even win me fair and square, Zack. You cheated."

"Yeah. Well, all's fair in love and cards."

He reached the top of the stairs, entered her room and tossed her unceremoniously on the bed.

"Zack, blow out the candle, please."

"No, I never make love with the lights out. Part of my enjoyment is the visual feast."

"Never?"

"Never."

"Oh."

"Does that disturb you?"

More than you can imagine, Victoria thought, but didn't say anything.

"The candle stays lit," Zack insisted. "Is that okay with you, Victoria?"

She nodded agreement.

He walked over to the bed and stood there watching her. Watching as she looked at his body and turned herself on with her thoughts as she had that first night in Desperado's.

"Well?" he said pensively.

"Well?" she echoed, puzzled.

"Are you gonna get naked or am I gonna have to give you real intense incentive?" He eased down the zipper on his jeans.

He wasn't kidding.

He kicked aside his jeans and stood with his hands on his hips. Victoria was too much woman to have that much virility blatantly challenging her and not respond to it.

The room was plenty light, with the candle flickering shadows on the wall. There could be no doubt about who was in the room with her this night. She went to Zack wearing the full gauzy skirt and pretty camisole top with pale ribbon ties at the shoulders that she'd slipped on before coming downstairs earlier.

Zack pulled her to him. As he cradled her against his groin a growl of pleasure erupted from his throat.

Victoria's hands were clasped behind his neck as she arched her back and leaned away from him. His lips moved hungrily to the tips of her breasts, dampening them through the thin cotton camisole.

A moan of surprise escaped her lips when she felt a second mouth slide down her neck to her nape in a sensual caress. But there was no one else in the room. Unless...

Johnny Bolero.

There's no such thing as ghosts, she assured herself as

those lips slid along her shoulder and then tugged at the ribbon anchored there.

The candle flickered and sputtered. Zack was kissing her, his hands anchored in her hair...while another man's hands were on her bare breasts, caressing, making her mind and senses reel.

She felt herself slipping into madness as an overload of intense pleasure overwhelmed her. In her inexperience, she couldn't say for sure if this was really happening. Maybe her imagination had run completely out of control. She couldn't catch her breath, much less hang on to a train of thought.

Her eyes closed and she couldn't tell if it was Zack or her ghostly lover whose lips were lathing her breasts, whose hands slipped beneath her skirt, whose lips were kissing the inside of her knees and inching upward.

The sensation of two men loving her at once was overwhelming, confusing. Nevertheless, she felt herself being sucked into the maelstrom of passion.

7

"NO!" VICTORIA CRIED, abruptly coming to her senses.

"No?" Zack raised his head from her breasts to look into her eyes. "Did I do something wrong?" he asked, looking puzzled and grudgingly insecure.

"No," she tried to assure him. "It's not you. It's me. I'm not ready.... Today has been so unsettling. I—I'm sorry Zack. I just can't. Not here."

"Not here?"

"No. Don't—touch me," she pleaded.

"But I'm *not* touching you," Zack said, exasperated.

Victoria stared at his hands; he was gesturing, palms up.

She considered explaining, but realized how ridiculous it would sound to him if she tried to say she hadn't been talking to him. How could she explain that she hadn't meant for *Zack* to quit touching her.

"Zack, I want to leave this place now. No questions, please. Let's just leave right now, okay?"

"If that's what you really want."

"Please don't be angry with me. I can't explain...." And she really couldn't, unless she wanted him to think he'd fallen in love with a crazy woman.

"Finish packing," he said, gesturing toward her suitcase. "When you're ready, meet me downstairs."

"No!"

"Now what?"

"I don't want to be alone in this room," she insisted, throwing all her things haphazardly into her suitcase.

"Where will we go next?" Zack asked, his expression telling her that his anger had cooled.

"I want to go home. I don't want to see any more ghost towns...ever."

"Are you all right?" he asked solicitously.

"Yes. I'm fine...really. Just humor me. Please." She wasn't fine. She was afraid she was going crazy.

When she finished packing, Zack lifted the suitcase from the bed and she followed him down the stairs and into the saloon, where she helped him clean up. When they'd eliminated any evidence that they had been there, she sat on the wooden bench outside the saloon and watched as Zack walked up and down the street of Pitchfork, making sure all the buildings were locked and everything was in order.

He probably thought she'd taken leave of her senses, and Victoria wasn't entirely sure he was wrong. All she knew was that telling him she'd seen a ghost...well, not seen, but worse...wouldn't help matters.

When Zack returned, his earlier scowl had been replaced by a concerned frown. "Are you starting to have second thoughts about Paul?" he asked abruptly.

"Paul? Oh, no."

"Then what's wrong? Tell me," he demanded, frustration wrinkling his strong brow.

"It's nothing. Really. I just need some time to think."

"You *are* having second thoughts," Zack declared.

"Zack, you have to admit the past few days have been emotionally exhausting. We *both* need time to think."

She could see Zack's fierce pride asserting itself as he agreed, "Perhaps you're right."

They continued to the car in silence—a silence that only grew deeper after they got under way.

Victoria worried about her state of mind. She knew she hadn't fantasized Johnny Bolero being the room with them. But by "knowing" it, didn't that mean she was in worse shape than she'd thought?

ZACK'S THOUGHTS TUMBLED over each other. What had gone wrong? One minute Victoria had been melting in his arms and the next she had turned to ice. Was it because she'd thought of Paul?

The way Zack saw it, he had two days and a night to erase any doubts that might have surfaced in Victoria's mind. He intended to take every advantage of that time, especially the night. He did his best work at night. Hadn't this morning just proven that? he thought with rueful humor.

The possibility suddenly occurred to him that Victoria could be innocent despite her simmering sensuality, which would explain her sudden balking at love-making. It would also explain there being no trace of Paul in her apartment. It wasn't something Zack could ask her straight out; she'd be furious. He didn't want her any more upset than she already was.

As always happened, the drive back seemed shorter, and Kansas City loomed on the horizon at the end of the day before he was ready, before he had a plan. He needed a plan. He rummaged around in his mind for an idea and remembered the intimate dinner he and Victoria had shared at the Mexican restaurant. Maybe if he took her back there, things between them would be okay again.

He broke into Victoria's thoughts. "I happen to know of this great restaurant in this town. I haven't had Mexican food in days and I'm going through withdrawal...." He raised his eyebrows hopefully.

Victoria glanced around her. "Since you're practically pulling into the parking lot already, it would be pointless for me to object. Mexican is fine."

Tonight's plan called for margaritas, and Zack ordered a pitcher as soon as they were seated in a small dark alcove.

"I'll just have a cola," Victoria told the waitress, foiling Zack's scheme.

When the waitress brought chips and salsa, Victoria ordered a salad. She didn't want to share anything with Zack. She wanted to keep as much distance between them as possible while she regained her equilibrium.

She had to keep telling herself there was no such thing as a ghost. Her fantasies had gotten way out of hand. She had to get a grip. Rational people didn't have fantasies they couldn't control.

When the waitress returned, Zack poured and drained a margarita to quench his thirst, getting up the nerve to confront Victoria with his feelings.

He wasn't sure how to broach the subject, and he'd only just worked up his nerve when he chanced to glance at the entrance to the restaurant. He groaned. "Great."

"What's the matter?" Victoria asked, following the path of his gaze. She saw two casually dressed young men wave and start bearing down on their table. "Do you know them, Zack?"

"Yeah, they're acquaintances of mine, sort of, from Los Angeles. They're doing stunt work on a movie in Kansas City. I'd forgotten. Well, it's too late to duck out now."

"Why would you want to duck out on your friends?" Victoria wondered. She didn't have to wonder long.

"Zack! What are you doing in this one-horse town? I thought you were set for the new Stallone movie." The wiry, redheaded man greeted Zack as if he'd known him forever, and his companion waited expectantly beside Victoria for an invitation to join them.

"They haven't started shooting yet," Zack replied, making no move to invite them to sit down.

"Why don't you introduce us?" asked the blond man with the crewcut, staring pointedly at the wedding ring on Victoria's finger.

Zack looked disinclined to do that, so Victoria introduced herself and asked the two men to join them, signaling the waitress to take their orders. She was suddenly full of energy and looking forward to whatever knowledge she could glean from Zack's two friends.

"So how do you all know each other? Have you been in movies together?" she queried, assuming from their lean, muscular bodies that the pair were stuntmen like Zack.

The redhead was full of information and only too happy to share it, which seemed to exacerbate Zack's sullen mood. The man regaled Victoria with anecdotes of their stuntmen antics as Zack listened without comment, glowering at his friends and slowly draining the pitcher of margaritas.

Finally the less talkative blond guy angered Zack by saying, "So you should be honored, Victoria. You're the first married lady I've ever seen Zack with. Not that he doesn't attract the married ones. But he's always resisted them and their requests." There was a knowing inflection in the word *requests*.

"But I'm not marr—" Victoria's denial was cut off when Zack grabbed her arm and threw some bills down on the table. "That should take care of our share. It's late and we've got some unfinished business to take care of," he said in a tone that dismissed both men.

Not wanting to create a scene, Victoria allowed Zack to hustle her out of the restaurant before she lit into him. "Of all the rude, insufferable..." She struggled to disengage her arm from his grasp.

"Yes, they were, weren't they? I apologize, but there's more than a little jealousy in Hollywood. But let's don't talk about them. You and I have unfinished business to take care of."

Outside in the night air, without the distraction of Zack's friends, Victoria belatedly noticed that Zack was tipsy. He wasn't falling-down drunk, but he was in no condition to drive a car. She hoped he wasn't going to be difficult about it. "Right now I think we need a place to stay for the night. Why don't you try to sleep off that pitcher of margaritas you drank while scowling at your friends, and I'll drive?"

Zack surprised her by giving her a little, mock salute and dropping the keys into her palm. She poured him inside the car and slid behind the wheel. Now for a place to stay the night. She knew nothing about Kansas City and didn't feel like driving around the city searching for accommodations with a tipsy man beside her. So she came to the reluctant decision that the easiest choice would be the motel they had stayed at on the way out, since it was nearby and familiar, if somewhat tacky. Okay, awfully tacky.

She left Zack sleeping in the car while she registered

and then woke him as she pulled up outside the unit number on the key in her hand.

"Zack, come on. Wake up," Victoria pleaded, shaking him gently.

Zack merely shrugged her hands away as if she were a pesky fly.

This was ridiculous, she thought. All she needed was for someone to come by and see her trying to coax an unwilling man into a motel room. How did she get herself into these situations? Why did Zack look so innocent when he was asleep? Must be because she couldn't see what was going on behind those dark, devilish eyes of his, she surmised.

Not only did he look innocent, he looked inviting. Victoria felt the lure of his sensual beauty, and before she realized what she was doing, she leaned over to nuzzle the indentation between his ear and his mouth.

There was absolutely no response. How was she going to get him out of the car and into the hotel room? She raked her teeth along his earlobe. No response. She slid her furled tongue into his ear and Zack's eyes blinked open. "Okay, I'm awake!"

Damn, just when she was beginning to enjoy herself. "Well, if you're awake, maybe you can make it to your room with only a little assistance from me?"

"Assistance? Are you kidding? I don't need assistance. I'm sober as a judge," he answered haughtily, and then proceeded to demonstrate his point. When he stumbled getting out of the car, he looked at her sheepishly. "Well, maybe I could use just a little assistance."

VICTORIA LET ZACK lean on her as she unlocked the door to Unit 6. The room had the same tacky decor as the one they'd shared on the way to Pitchfork. Victoria knew she was in worse shape than she'd suspected when it dawned on her that the tasteless room was starting to look like home to her.

Zack stretched out across the round bed and smiled sheepishly. "I knew it all along," he mumbled. "You really do like this place."

Victoria shook her head and went to retrieve her luggage from the car. She let herself into the unit next door, locked the door behind her and leaned back against it with a sigh. Time alone to think at last.

She glanced around the gaudy room.

Truly alone.

No self-respecting ghost would be caught dead in this room, she decided, then chuckled at the insanity of that thought.

She went to take a shower, pleased to find there was a massage showerhead. She turned the dial to let the warm water pound the tension from her back. Stepping from the enclosure, she grabbed a towel to blot the dampness from her skin, then slipped into the pink, frothy nightgown she'd pulled from her suitcase.

Zack's fragrance kept drifting up to her, as if the short gown she had on had been handled by him.

She'd been so sure she'd drift right off to sleep, but instead she lay awake remembering the night she'd spent with Zack in an identical unit.

Was that when she'd fallen in love with him? Or was it the first time their eyes had met at Desperado's? But she was being fanciful, and she'd promised herself she'd stop being fanciful.

Still, there was no doubt in her mind that she wanted to marry Zack. She realized now that it wasn't just the dark-eyed scoundrels who were dangerous. Paul had proven that even nice guys would take a woman for granted, given half a chance. But a woman had to *allow* herself to be taken for granted, and Victoria had no intention of letting that happen. As for being in love...well, sometimes you just had to close your eyes, take a deep breath and plunge right in. Sometimes the reward was worth the risk.

That still left the problem of Johnny. Victoria knew she didn't *have* to tell Zack about him; the subject would probably never come up. Pitchfork was behind them now. But she wanted Zack to know. She had to tell someone, or go crazy. So in the morning she would confide in him and find out if he was willing to marry a crazy lady.

The phone rang, loud, startling and shrill in the dark, silent room. She picked up the receiver and listened.

"Hi. Enjoying the movie?" Zack asked softly.

"Movie?"

"That *is* why you checked us into this place, isn't it?

At first I thought you had designs on my body and were going to take advantage of me while I was tipsy and compliant. But when you abandoned me, I remembered how much you liked the movies they show here."

Victoria hung up on him, but not before hearing his laughter.

MINUTES LATER the phone rang again and Victoria ignored it. Zack refused to hang up, letting it ring until she answered in self-defense.

"Hi," he said innocently.

"Zack, I want to get some sleep."

"Then why are you watching a movie?"

"I'm *not* watching a movie!"

"What do you have on?"

"What do I have on?"

"Did I say 'repeat after me'?"

"Zack!"

"You don't have *anything* on?"

"Of course I have something on. I've got on my pink..."

"The pink...ah, my favorite...it's so sheer you might as well be naked."

"How do you know? What did you do, go through my luggage?"

"I didn't mean to. I opened your suitcase by accident."

"Zack, it's after midnight." Victoria was losing patience. "What do you want?"

"I want to know what's wrong with me."

"What are you talking about?"

"You know what I'm talking about. Back in Pitchfork."

"Zack, that had nothing to do with you."

"Right. There were only the two of us in the room and it had nothing to do with me."

"Zack, this isn't the time to be discussing it."

Zack's voice grew soft. "Victoria, don't ask me to face you and ask you why I don't measure up as a lover."

Victoria heard the pain in his voice. She had to explain. "Zack, I'm telling you it wasn't you...it was...Johnny."

"Johnny? Who the hell is Johnny?"

"A ghost."

"What?"

"Remember the poster on the wall, of the gunfighter who owned the saloon? His name was Johnny Bolero, remember? I know this sounds crazy, but I'm sure he was in the room with us."

Zack swore. "You mean you went cold on me because you thought a ghost was in the room, watching us?"

"Not just watching."

"Not just watching...what the hell else do ghosts do?"

"Just forget it, Zack. I knew you wouldn't believe me."

"Look, Victoria, I know you're imaginative. You admit it yourself. So what's so terrible about a ghost being in the room while I'm loving you? It's a little kinky maybe." He laughed as if he couldn't believe what he'd just said.

"Zack, I think he believes I'm his Sara. When you were kissing me..." Lord, if he thought *watching* was kinky...

"What?"

"I could feel his caress on my body." There, it was out. She'd told him. She waited for his hoot of laughter.

"*That's* when you froze in my arms?"

"Yes."

There was a long silence on Zack's end of the line.

"Zack, are you still there?" Victoria asked tentatively.

"Yes. I'm thinking."

"Thinking I'm crazy, right?" Victoria was getting worried.

There was a long, nerve-racking pause, then he said, "Crazy is a relative term. I'm *crazy* about you. Do you trust me?"

"Yes."

"Still going to marry me?" Zack asked, and there was silence, as if he was holding his breath.

"Yes." Victoria looked around her, not believing she had just accepted a marriage proposal in this tacky room. It was probably the first decent proposal the room had ever witnessed.

Zack wasn't quite finished with his proposal. "Marry me in Pitchfork?"

"Pitchfork?"

"Yes."

She'd marry him anywhere. "But why Pitchfork?"

"Because I have a score to settle with Johnny Bolero," he said. "Maybe we're both crazy, but I felt something in Pitchfork, too. Something I still can't explain. I just know we need to go back."

VICTORIA SPENT the following day at Country Club Plaza shopping for clothes while Zack was off making his mysterious plans.

It was a beautiful warm night and he met her for dinner at Nabils. The wrought-iron balconies and intricate gate was a romantic backdrop for outdoor dining. After feasting on Kansas City's famous steak they toasted their impending nuptials with champagne that tickled Victoria's nose and gave her hiccups.

No matter how hard she pressed Zack to reveal his plans for their Pitchfork wedding, he wouldn't break his silence. He continued to insist it was a surprise, a wedding gift. He wouldn't budge.

"So tell me, what exactly did you buy for your trousseau today?" Zack asked as they left the restaurant.

"Uh-uh, that's *my* surprise."

ZACK HAILED a horse-drawn carriage and they rode down Wornall Road, enjoying the sights and simply being snuggled together. Though the chemistry between them still burned as brightly as ever, there was a quiet new love and understanding between them.

Zack instructed the driver of their horse and carriage to stop at the Neptune Fountain when Victoria said she wanted to toss a coin and make a wish.

After she had done so, she and Zack took off their shoes to wade in the water around the statue of Neptune. They frolicked like children, finding release from the high intensity of their time in Pitchfork.

Zack surprised her with the fact that he'd reserved a room for them at the Plaza, but their agreement not to sleep together remained in force.

After relaxing in the hot tub, they went to bed, where Zack fell into a restful sleep, his breathing even.

Victoria didn't drop off so easily.

Her agreement that they not sleep together until they returned to Pitchfork had been made because she knew it was important to Zack.

As she lay beside him, watching him sleep, her mind wasn't on the purest of thoughts. She wondered what he would do if she ravished him in his sleep. Could a woman ravish a man? She certainly felt up to it.

Eventually she, too, dozed off. But it was a fitful sleep.

8

IT WAS LATE AFTERNOON when Victoria and Zack pulled into Pitchfork. The sun was starting its slip toward the horizon, and the old man Victoria remembered from the creek was sitting on the bench outside the Silver Spur Saloon. Two men, looking tired and dusty, leaned against the hitching post.

"What are they doing here?" Victoria asked, surprised by the welcoming committee.

"The old-timer is a friend of mine. The other two are of his choosing. I needed them for a chore that was long overdue."

"You know the old man?"

"Yes, but I'll explain all that later. Right now I have a score to settle with Johnny Bolero. The three of them should have everything set up by now."

Victoria acquiesced, amazed at herself for going along with his scheme when he was keeping her in the dark.

"So is one of them a parapsychologist?" she ventured, eyeing the three men.

"Not quite." Zack chuckled. "What we have here are a minister and two witnesses." He came around and opened the car door for her.

"Don't tell me the old man is a minister?" Victoria said incredulously. He was the most likely of the three because he was wearing a suit. Or at least he was wearing his idea of a suit.

"Semiretired. There's a young minister, but Mr. Parsons... Swear to God," Zack said, laughing at her disbelieving look. "Mr. Parsons handles the occasional chore in the next town when the young minister is too busy."

They reached the boardwalk in front of the saloon, where Mr. Parsons was waiting with outstretched hands to greet them. "Howdy. This here be Luke and Zeke," he said, indicating the two dusty men.

"Mr. Parsons, I'd like you to meet my fiancée, Victoria Stone," Zack said.

"Oh, we've already met," the old-timer said. "I may be old, but I never forget a pretty gal."

"Help yourself, boys, to the cold drinks in the cooler in the trunk of the car," Zack said, tossing Luke the keys. "Mr. Parsons, we should be ready in about a half hour, if that's okay with you."

"That'd be just fine. Main thing is we finish up before sunset."

Mr. Parsons had picked up his Bible and was paging through it as Victoria and Zack went into the saloon.

"This is going to make an unusual wedding, to say the least," Victoria said.

"Even more unusual than you think," Zack said. "I want you to wear the red satin dress."

"The one I barely fit into?" Victoria exclaimed.

"Do your bridegroom a favor and humor me. Besides, I thought it fit great."

"I can imagine what Zeke and Luke will think," Victoria muttered as she followed Zack upstairs. She looked out the window, down onto the dusty street, as she waited for Zack to fetch the dress.

"Are you sure about this?" Victoria asked when he returned and handed her the red satin.

"Please?" he asked plaintively.

Victoria could see Zack's eyes were going to get him his way often. "Okay," she agreed, silently thankful there would be no pictures.

Zack left her alone to dress and returned for her in half an hour. He knocked at her door. "Ready, Victoria?"

She'd been ready for Zack DeLuca all her life. Taking one last tug at the plunging neckline of the red satin dress he'd insisted on, she went to join him.

He was dressed in the same snug black pants he'd found that first night in the saloon, and he'd added a black shirt and kerchief. He could have walked right off a Johnny Bolero Wanted poster, Victoria thought, gulping for air.

They looked anything but traditional as they went down the stairs to join Mr. Parsons and his two friends. "Well, don't you make a fine pair," Mr. Parsons said with a wide smile of approval. Zeke and Luke were falling all over themselves to look at Victoria's cleavage without being caught.

"Where do you want to say the words?" the minister asked, Bible in his hand. He breathed a sigh of relief when he saw the bookmark had stayed in place.

Zack took Victoria's hand in his. "At the top of the hill where the wildflowers are."

The little wedding party of five made its way to the site Zack had indicated.

Victoria saw that someone had righted Sara Pritchard's headstone, and when they got closer she was surprised to see a fresh grave next to Sara's.

She looked at Zack questioningly.

"I found Sara's grave when I came up here to pick those wildflowers for your pillow," he said. "I knew Johnny Bolero was buried in the town, where he'd been killed in a gunfight. Sara's parents probably wouldn't hear of him being buried next to her, blaming him for their daughter's death. I've had Mr. Parsons taking care of the necessary paperwork to have the remains moved." Zack turned to the minister and asked anxiously, "Mr. Parsons, are you ready?"

Victoria was amused by the old-timer, who was practically beaming as he started the marriage ceremony. The words were familiar and reassuring until he startled Victoria by saying, "Do you, Johnny Bolero, take this woman to be your lawful wedded wife?" Her eyes grew wide with understanding that it was a proxy wedding, albeit a very unusual one. Then it was her turn, and Mr. Parsons said, "Do you, Sara Pritchard, take this man to be your lawful wedded husband?"

There were tears in her eyes when the ceremony was over and Zack slipped the once-tight gold wedding band from her finger. Reaching down and scooping up a few handfuls of dirt, he buried the ring between the graves, its inscription now true.

"That's what you call settling the score?" Victoria asked through a blur of tears, a sniffle in her voice.

"Damn straight. Johnny brought my bride to me. The least I could was return the favor."

THE SUN DIPPED DOWN low over the horizon as Zack pulled her into his arms for the wedding kiss. Zeke and Luke avoided looking at the mushy nonsense, while Mr. Parsons gazed upon the couple with benevolent satisfaction.

The little party made its way back down the hill and disbanded after Zack paid them for their help.

He then turned to Victoria and wiped the tears still clinging to her cheeks with his thumbs. "Do you always cry at weddings?" he asked.

"Only when they are wildly romantic," she answered, loving him for what he'd done. Paul would have thought she was crazy, but not Zack.

"You mean I'm gonna have to buy you a drip-dry wedding gown?" he teased.

"What do you mean?" she asked.

"For when we do it up proper, when we get back."

Zack placed his hand on Victoria's back and took her into the Silver Spur Saloon. "I don't think however," he continued, "that we should leave Pitchfork without having a bit of a honeymoon." Positioning her by the cherry-wood bar, he lifted her effortlessly, settling her atop it.

"What are you doing?" she asked.

"I want this to be memorable. Given your penchant for western ghost towns, it follows you would have a thing for cowboys." He lifted a white Stetson from the end of the bar and settled it on his head. "Recognize me? I'm the good guy." He grinned wickedly. "The *really* good guy."

Victoria laughed, her eyes wide. "You mean right here? On the bar?"

His grin stayed in place as he nodded. "Kind of gives a whole new twist to the phrase belly up to the bar, now doesn't it?"

"Zack!"

"Get used to it. I plan to shock your socks off tonight—in the very nicest way, of course. I'm not just some drifter, ma'am. I'm here to stay."

Victoria had thought he'd never ask. And it was going to be pretty hard to shock her socks off. Though she was inexperienced, it was true, she had a very lively imagination.

Zack kissed her then, unleashing a reckless hunger that had been restrained for too long. He could feel her accelerated pulse against his thumb as he held her head, cradling it in his probing kiss.

Was she feeling the same raw desire? he wondered. Was it possible for one so inexperienced? Should he go slow as he'd planned or respond to her eagerness?

Slow. Slow, he decided, was the safe way to go. He didn't want to blow this. He wanted it to be perfect for Victoria. It was almost always better slow.

And he wanted it to last.

If he could. He was so ready for her, ready to sheath himself in her hot, silken body. The black pants that had started out snug were now supremely uncomfortable.

His breathing was labored as he broke their kiss.

He wanted them naked. Skin to skin.

And when they were, he lit the candles on the bar. Their soft light flickered in the dusky saloon.

She was naked—completely—down to the desire he saw flickering in her eyes. And he'd shed his good-guy white hat with his clothes, but she'd insisted he leave the black kerchief.

When he hoisted himself up on the bar to join her, she tugged the black kerchief up to cover the bottom half of his face. "There now, you look like the robber who's come to steal my virginity."

He felt the kerchief flutter at his confident laugh. "Love, when I'm done with you, you're going to be offering me your most valuable possession and begging me to take it. It's going to be easy as skinny-dipping on a hot day. You want that cooling dip so much you don't care who knows—or sees."

He turned her on her side so she could see them in the huge mirror behind the bar, their naked bodies bathed in golden candlelight. The reflection was erotic and compelling.

With his free hand he began exploring her body while she watched in fascination.

"This is incredibly sexy, but not the most comfortable spot in town," Victoria said, smiling warmly at his reflection. "I think my hip just fell asleep."

"Don't worry, I'll wake up every inch of you." With that he reached out and picked up something from behind the bar.

"What are you planning to do with that?" she asked, her eyes wide and a bit wary.

"Why, wake you up, of course."

He began trailing the silver spur ever so gently over her hips, moving on to other, more sensually charged spots on her body, knowing the cowboy item would excite her.

She didn't comment, only moaned.

Gradually halting the foreplay with the silver spur, Zack insisted she was too keyed up, too tense. He maneuvered her until she was facedown on the bar, then began an expert massage not meant to relax her at all. His devilish laughter gave him away as he worked magic with his hands, kneading and rubbing and working his way down her back from her shoulders and neck.

Past her waist.

He knew exactly the effect he was causing when his hands cupped her bottom and stroked and squeezed.

"I want to turn over," Victoria groaned in a muffled voice.

"Not yet," he replied, fueling her pleasure, showing her he really was a good guy, with his hands at least. Really good.

And then he inched her legs apart so his fingertips grazed her, just close enough to her mounting, wanting sensations to tantalize, to build her passion, to make her cry out.

"Okay, okay, you can turn over," he said with a swat to her bottom, followed by a kiss before he helped her to face him. Her skin was flushed to a sexy rosy hue.

He kissed her lips, denying her demands, cutting off her requests. Tonight they would do things his way. There was plenty of time to let her teach him what she wanted. And he would be only too glad to learn.

Looking down at her, he couldn't resist teasing, "Hold on tight, it just might be a very bumpy ride up here and we wouldn't want to fall off the bar, sweetheart." Positioning himself over her, he eased his hardness into her very slowly, expecting difficulty.

There was only a little.

Victoria gave a small cry and then began squirming

beneath him, tugging him to her, urging him to please her.

All his carefully laid plans for taking it slow and easy fell away as he began drowning in the sensations of passion her desire brought to him.

Smooth, steady and fast, they climbed together until satisfaction swept over them, quenching their immediate fever.

Both of them knew, however, that the night was young.

9

VICTORIA AND ZACK LAY in the four-poster bed listening to the soft rain that had begun to fall. She studied the intricate pattern of the old quilt in the soft light of the candle on the dressing table as she thought back over the events of the day and evening. She took Zack's hand and squeezed it. "That was a dear thing you did, arranging the proxy marriage for Sara and Johnny."

He squeezed her hand back. "Thank you, darling. You might be surprised to learn that I, too, have always had a fascination for gunslingers. Unlike you, however, I fantasized I *was* one. I had the same feelings of déjà vu that you did here in Pitchfork.

"I discovered the place when I was doing research for a script I'm writing and producing. Much as I hate to admit it, I can't be a stuntman forever. One of these days these bones are gonna start getting crinks."

"I'd say that's a long way into the future, judging by your 'bartending' performance."

He chuckled. "I've spent my vacations for the past couple of years driving around researching the background for *Fast Draw*. I heard about Pitchfork being restored through the show-business grapevine, and when Paul told me about your vacation plans, I put him together with the movie people and arranged for you to visit before shooting started."

"How did you get the idea for *Fast Draw?*" she asked, turning to kiss his cheek affectionately.

"A dream," he replied, hugging her to him.

"A dream?"

"I'm afraid it was inspired by the legend of Johnny Bolero. I saw the gunfight in my dream."

It gave Victoria an eerie chill to think that they'd had such similar dreams, perhaps even the same dream.

"Talking to people like that old-timer you met, Mr. Parsons, I saw how Pitchfork must have been in its heyday. Since action is what I know, I plan to use Johnny Bolero's real-life story as the connecting thread between a series of spectacular stunts." What he didn't tell her was that he intended to play the part of Johnny Bolero. Zack felt it was a role he was meant to play.

"I do love you. I can't believe how much," Victoria said, nuzzling closer. "I think our love was fated."

"Maybe," he agreed. And they lay together listening to the rain until Zack drifted off to sleep.

She hoped he was sleeping soundly, because she was restless as a baby in church. Remembering that her big suitcase, which was still in the trunk of the car, had a paperback novel in it, she slid out of bed and picked up the candle from the dressing table. She considered waking up Zack but then decided that was foolish.

Making her way downstairs, she watched all kinds

of shadows float eerily against the walls. She swore softly when she got to the car. Why hadn't she thought about the trunk being locked? She was going to have to wake Zack.

She climbed the stairs again, going to the room where Zack was asleep. He wasn't snoring, but then maybe he didn't snore. He hadn't at the motel. In the candle's glow she could see the even pattern of his breathing.

The black pants he'd worn were lying across the foot of the bed. If she was quiet she should be able to slip his keys from his pants without waking him. She took one last look at the angular face she loved—so innocent in sleep, with a dark shadow of a beard already showing. Inhaling deeply, she leaned across the bed and slid her hand into the pocket of his pants.

"I've been lying here hoping you'd want to get in my pants again. But this wasn't what I had in mind."

The sheet covering him cleared his body with a flick of his wrist.

As fast as Johnny Bolero's gun must have cleared his holster.

"I'd say this is hard evidence that I want you, wouldn't you?"

The man was insatiable. What had she gotten herself into? Yes, indeed what.

She watched spellbound as Zack clamped his hand around her wrist and pulled her to sit beside him on the bed. He released his grip, then instructed her to touch him.

Victoria's hand opened and closed on the bed at her side, but she didn't move toward him.

Zack rimmed her tremulous lips with his thumb. "Pleasure me. I love you so. I want to feel your touch."

Victoria edged her hand toward him tentatively, stopping nervously to caress his thigh.

"That's a good start," he said, his tumescence straining toward her fingers. Slowly she raised her hand and wrapped it loosely around him, her touch tentative and uncertain.

Zack groaned and closed his eyes in sensual delight.

He was a dichotomy of soft steel beneath her touch. Growing more confident and enjoying the surge of feminine power his enjoyment gave her, she began moving her hand, feeling the wiry brush of his dark body hair against her wrist. Zack leaned back on his elbow, and his body tensed as her hand slid over him. His head was thrown back, his neck arched, and sweat began to sheen on his flat belly, making the back of Victoria's hand slick.

She let go of him to wipe her hand on the sheet, and when she grasped him again he guided her. With his fingers covering hers, he showed her the exact pressure, controlled her movements. It was intimacy and sharing, exquisite in its tenderness and trust. When he growled her name, warning of his release, she reveled in the sound of his voice. Never had her name sounded so very special. Never had it been said with such love.

He made no move to touch her, even to kiss her. He opened his eyes at last. They were glazed with pleasure and love as he looked at her. A slow, lazy grin spread over his face. "Thank you, ma'am," he said, tipping his imaginary hat, showing her there was a place for laughter in the most private of moments. "I'm sure I'd never have survived the night if you hadn't been so kind." He grew serious then and said, "I'd never have allowed any other woman to do that."

10

IT HAD BEEN HOURS since Victoria had melted from his side.

A smile of satisfaction wreathed Zack's face. *Victoria DeLuca,* he thought, trying to imagine what their child would look like when they had one. Tried to imagine a toddler's face with Victoria's pale eyes and his dark coloring. He wasn't without vanity. The child—a girl—would be beautiful. Someday she would be a prima ballerina.

His mind was back on stuntwork and he began to think about *Fast Draw.* He staged a gunfight in his mind. It would require consummately skilled stuntmen, for he wanted to do the first part of the gunfight in slow motion, reflecting the telescoping of time, the horror a person feels watching such an event. Then the movie would speed up to show the terrible skill of a deadly quick draw as the gunfighter picked off secondary guns like bottles on a fence rail. The lighting would be important, too. He made a mental note to himself to spotlight each gunfighter and then dash the light to show the light that goes out of the world at each person's death.

He was too rested to sleep. The rain outside had ceased its lulling patter and had slowed to a misty drizzle. He was full of energy—ridiculous for this time of night. He felt like...like practicing the quick draw he would need to play Johnny Bolero. Later he would train with an expert, but tonight he could store up memories, atmosphere.... It would give him a base if he soaked up how it felt to face an opponent on a dirt street in the old West. And it appealed to the romantic in him...the performer in him...the child.

He pulled on the black pants, which still lay at the foot of the bed, and headed downstairs, feeling like a teenager slipping out to do mischief. He cussed as his toe came into combat with a chair, and carefully avoided having it happen again, picking his way gingerly through the obstacles as he headed toward the saloon's swinging doors.

He knew where he could get a pistol and holster to practice with. Outside, the smooth surface of the unpaved street, damp now with the rain, reminded him he was barefoot as he crossed to the barbershop. He picked the lock easily, and there on a peg was the holster and pistol he remembered. He lifted them and as an afterthought picked up the black Stetson hanging nearby. He shoved the hat on his head with a rueful smile and thought of boys and their toys as he buckled on the holster on his way out. The drizzle had stopped and the mist was clearing. Moonlight bathed the street in an eerie light.

Standing with feet apart, Zack tipped back his Stetson to stare down his invisible opponent. With deliberate intimidation he pushed back an imaginary long slicker. His smile was as deadly as his aim. He was doing his own narrative in his head, he found to his amusement.

His legs spread in a macho stance. He felt his pelvis tilt forward aggressively as he really got into the role. He decided to draw on the count of three. One...he shifted the imaginary cigarette to the other side of his mouth. Two...he held his hands curved out at his sides in poised readiness. Three...he cleared the holster so unexpectedly quickly that he lost control of the pistol and it flew out of his hand, arcing and tumbling to the damp street.

He laughed in delight. He was good! Damn straight he was. He picked up the pistol with wonder. Where had this natural ability come from? Was it just good reflexes, or... He picked up the gun and slid it back into the holster that hung low on his hips.

The dancer in him took over and he began making running leaps and whirling, pulling the gun from the holster before he landed on his feet, making an imaginary fanning motion with his hand. The gun was unloaded, of course, so he had an endless supply of "bullets."

He drew the gun slowly and felt the weight of it in his hand. It felt very comfortable, though he'd never held a gun before, to his knowledge—not even a toy one. He'd been at dancing class when boys his age had been playing cowboys, yet the gun felt as comfortable to him as his dancing tights once had.

Feeling the exhilaration of the moment, he became acrobatic, doing running tumbles with the gun in his hand, then firing from the crouched position. It was during one of these tumbles that he caught the flicker of a curtain in a window above the saloon. Was Victoria watching him? He imagined he looked pretty silly. He glanced down at his bare chest and feet and the snug black pants bisected by the low-slung gun belt, its leather ties anchoring the holstered gun to his hard thigh. He picked up the black Stetson, which hadn't made it through his first tumble, and saluted the window before settling it back on his head and dusting himself off. There was no acknowledgment from the window. It had been his imagination.

Once he'd worn himself out, he felt his griminess. He needed a bath. He dug the keys from his pocket and unlocked the trunk of his car. Riffling through his suitcase revealed the fact that he'd used up all his fresh towels. He turned to Victoria's big suitcase and opened it. He swore she had brought enough towels for three baths a day.

After grabbing a warm beer from the bar and lighting another candle, he made his way upstairs without bashing any of his precious toes. Victoria had fallen asleep in a chair while reading. He lifted the paperback novel that lay open on her chest. It was titled, appropriately, *Gunslinger's Señorita.*

If it had been her at the window, and not a figment of his imagination, she didn't want him to know it. He smiled indulgently and went to the dresser, feeling as grimy as a cowboy who had been herding steers all day. After taking a whiff of his armpits, he decided he smelled like one of the steers. He set Victoria's book and the beer on the table beside the bed. Unbuckling the gun belt and untying the rawhide strap from his thigh, he placed it and the Stetson on the foot of the bed, to be returned to the barbershop in the morning.

Settling into the warm water of the old-fashioned tub, he soaked for a while, then soaped up until his tanned skin was squeaky clean. He got out of the tub and dried off, peering at his reflection in the antique mirror over the washstand. He studied his beard, which he'd let grow for several days. It would have to stay. He had only brought an electric razor, and while modern plumbing had been added to the ghost town for the movie company's convenience, they hadn't gone so far as to install electricity—they'd bring their own generators.

He returned to the bedroom to find that while the bath had relaxed him, he was still energized by his workout on the street below. Setting down the candle and lying down on the bed, he took a sip of the beer and rested it on his stomach while studying the book that had been in Victoria's hands. Its cover was flamboyant, depicting a desperado with two rounds of ammunition strapped across his bare chest, a cowboy hat tilted rakishly over his forehead and black pants very similar to the ones Zack had been wearing earlier hugging his hips.

Zack laughed as he studied the art closer. The desperado didn't have a gun in his hand, but what he did have looked a lot more lethal. The señorita he was embracing was lush and far from retiring. She seemed to be defying him to do something. Exactly what, Zack couldn't put a name to.

Intrigued, he opened the cover and began reading. *My, my, my, my, my.* The book gave a whole new meaning to the term "Wild West." He lost himself in the story as the candle flickered lower and then an hour later guttered, the wick submerged in liquid wax.

Was it raining again? Was rain blowing in the open window onto his chest? But no, it was something else. He struggled to consciousness. Was a kitten washing him with its tongue? There it was, the wet again. He felt a little rivulet slide from his chest down over his ribs. He wrinkled his nose. He smelled beer. He reached down and his hand encountered soft curls.

It was a woman's curls and it was a woman's giggle he heard as she licked up the drops of beer she was sprinkling on his chest. He sighed with contentment, still half-asleep. Victoria had come to him. He murmured soft complaints like a dreaming puppy as she continued her play on his chest. Her tongue tormented him as she ran it over his ribs, following the errant trickles of beer that had gone exploring.

It was still dark outside and everything was shrouded in a foggy mist. He reached to light the candle and then remembered it had burned itself out. He gave up thoughts of seeing and lost himself in feeling, still in that languorous state of half sleep. Her tongue flicked the dark button of his nipple and a thrill raced along his spine. "You're insatiable, woman," he said around a very dry throat, sure now that it had been her at the window.

Her delicate finger slid vertically over his lips, indicating her desire that he be silent. She obviously didn't want to talk, but...well, he could get into what she wanted to do...was doing. *Ahh, Victoria,* he thought, careful not to say it aloud after her request for silence. Who did she think they were going to disturb, for heaven's sake? A smile played over his mouth as he let his hands wander. He'd never dreamed anything this good before; it had to be real.

The air stealing in through the window was moist and cool, yet somehow sultry. He placed his hands on her breasts, which were pouting in the air above him. He heard her breath catch as he flexed his long fingers in a squeezing caress. Her lips were soft as she moved his hand to her mouth and raked gentle teeth across his knuckles, while playfully darting her tongue between his fingers.

She slid her soft hands over his muscular arms and

made a sexy journey down through the sleek dark hair covering his chest. His body tensed under her tongue. The delightful sensation raced along his nerve endings, spreading urgent commands of fulfillment. His palms were damp as he placed them on her thighs and pulled her astride him, his hands gently insistent as he lifted her.

She controlled everything after that, pinning his hands to his sides playfully with her soft heels. Their breath intermingled as she slowly lowered herself on him, and he descended into the silky oblivion of pleasure. Since he was unable to use his hands, his mouth became ravenous on hers—soft, hot and intimate.

She responded by writhing against his body, her hands dawdling here and there as she stroked him. The thin sheen of perspiration covering both of them made the contact of skin on skin incredibly erotic. He pressed his aching flesh slowly, deeply into her, greedy to feel each tremor of her desire.

And then his hands broke free as, in her excitement, she relaxed the tension of her heels against him. She cried out and came in ecstasy as he slid his fingers up to touch her. His response to her climaxing against him was a half-strangled groan of lust. The fire building inside him refused boundaries and exploded in a ball of flame so intense she held her hand to his mouth to muffle his shout of joyous completion.

HE SLID INTO A DEEP SLEEP, embracing his woman in the crook of his arm, a smile on his lips.

When he woke in the morning, his mind was clear and he remembered nothing of the night before until he looked down and saw the empty beer can lying on its side next to his belly.

Everything came back to him in a rush—each image, each touch, all the emotions. But where was Victoria? Why had she left him? It had been real, hadn't it? He hadn't just fallen asleep with the beer in his hand and dreamed everything when the beer had overturned, had he?

He pulled on a pair of jeans, picked up the gun belt and hat he was going to return to the barbershop, and walked across the hall to where Victoria slept. Sunlight was slanting in her open window and across the quilt thrown over her legs. She didn't look as if she'd moved since he'd checked on her last night. Had he been dreaming? Or was Sara as restless as Johnny? Had Sara and Johnny been together at last through them?

Listen to him; he was becoming as fanciful as Victoria! He walked into the room. Setting the gun belt down on the bed, still holding the black Stetson, he sat down for a closer look. Victoria was flushed with sleep...or were those whisker burns on her cheeks?

He shook her gently, then with more force, when it was apparent to him she was sleeping soundly. At last she flung out her arms to resist waking, the action waking her.

"Wake up, sleepyhead," he said, watching as she rubbed her eyes like a small child.

"I refuse to wake up to someone grinning like a fool at the crack of dawn," Victoria answered querulously, stretching her arms above her head, then folding them across her chest at the mischievous glint playing in Zack's appreciative gaze.

"Do you by any chance walk in your sleep?" he asked, still puzzled over last night. He playfully dropped the black Stetson atop Victoria's head.

The Stetson was sizes too big and slipped down over her forehead, covering her eyes. "Oh, good, it's dark—it must be time to go to sleep again," she quipped gleefully, covering her yawn with one hand.

"You didn't answer my question," Zack said, not to be distracted, though she looked damn cute.

Victoria flipped the hat off and it landed upended on the bed between them. "No...once I fall asleep, I don't even move."

"Hmm...in that case I may withdraw my marriage proposal," Zack teased with innuendo.

"What's all this about walking in my sleep, anyway?" she asked, reaching for the hat as something sticking in the band inside caught her attention.

"Nothing," Zack replied, deciding he'd had an erotic dream and nothing more.

Victoria caught the corner of the picture stuck in the hat's lining. She pulled it free and brought it toward her for closer inspection. Her eyes widened.

"Zack...look at this!"

He moved closer to see what she was so excited about.

In her hand she held an old sepia photograph. The man in the picture wore the same black hat that now rested on her head. There was a woman beside him, and they were posing in front of the Silver Spur Saloon. The photograph had caught the love on their faces. It could have been Victoria and Zack, the resemblances were that close.

Victoria and Zack looked up from the picture and stared into each other's eyes and knew—knew the reason for the fantasies that had drawn them to Pitchfork. The man and the woman in the picture, the couple who were so obviously in love, were Victoria and Zack...when they'd been Sara and Johnny.

Their love was fated.

They were meant to be together again as more than a ghostly image.

11

Variety

Zack DeLuca is set to become the latest face to turn his physical skills into gold, following in the footsteps of action stars Stallone and Schwarzenegger. The former stuntman turned writer/producer will play the lead in *Fast Draw,* a new western, to be filmed in Pitchfork, Colorado.

National Enquirer

Zack DeLuca, starring in new western, *Fast Draw*, married his best friend's fiancée today. Best friend was not present at the quiet ceremony.

Billboard

"Outlaw Blues," the hot new single from the group Wild West, has been selected as the theme song for *Fast Draw,* the western that's drawing a lot of buzz in the film industry. Watch for "Outlaw Blues" to have a long ride on the charts if the movie opens big.

Movieline

Word is that shoot-'em-up *Fast Draw* had gone over budget and its star, Zack DeLuca, is responsible. Not good news. It seems the weather isn't cooperating, either. Pitchfork got an unexpected snowfall, which means more delays.

People

Flashbulbs popped tonight at the Los Angeles premiere of *Fast Draw.* Everyone including the star, Zack DeLuca, and his lovely wife were dressed for the occasion in western gear. DeLuca even wore spurs...maybe to ward off any reviewer's inclination to give a bad review.

Premiere

The success of *Fast Draw* has made Zack DeLuca Hollywood's newest It Boy. After opening #2 for the week at the box office, it's held on to become one of the season's biggest hits.

Denver Post

Pitchfork, Colorado, the restored ghost town where hit movie *Fast Draw* was filmed, has become one of Colorado's biggest tourist attractions. Let's hope Zack DeLuca films another feature in our state soon.

Variety

Fast Draw wins a Golden Globe award for its star, newcomer Zack DeLuca. Due to the movie's huge box-office success, three big-name directors have announced plans to film a western of their own.

People

Zack DeLuca, star of the movie *Fast Draw,* heads the list of *People* magazine's sexiest men in America. Women everywhere are waiting with baited breath for the announcement of his next movie.

Epilogue

SHE WATCHED HIM from her table as he stood talking with a group of young men in navy dress whites. She could see he was an officer, but a gentleman? Well, maybe. The handsomest of the group, he stood a little taller than the others, and as he leaned against the bar he seemed to feel her eyes on him.

When he looked her way, she quickly averted her gaze to one of the deco posters of seductive women that gave the club a certain sensual mood. Live music competed successfully with the clamor of the by-invitation-only party.

The cat-and-mouse game between them continued when she lifted her eyes to see him laugh at a remark one of the men in his group had made. He had to know what a rich, sexy laugh he had. A laugh that carried across the room to her as if it were a caress. She found herself smiling.

Of course, that was the moment he chose to turn his attention back to her.

He took her smile as an invitation and began detaching himself from the group.

He had her pinned with his gaze as he wove his way through the crowded club to her table, his white hat tucked under his arm. She wasn't the only one watching him approach. He was the kind of man who turned heads and garnered inviting smiles. No wonder he'd mistaken hers as such.

The band began playing "Outlaw Blues" as he leaned down to whisper his request for a dance in her ear. It wasn't so much a request as a demand. "They're playing our song."

How could she resist?

She couldn't and didn't.

She allowed him to usher her to the dance floor, his hand at her back protective, possessive.

"Outlaw Blues" was a slow song with a saxophone that wailed longingly. He pulled her in close and wrapped her hand in his. He let his body do the talking as they danced on the crowded floor. His warm breath tingled against her nape. The polished buttons on his uniform pushed against her through the celery green slip dress she wore.

It was very clear to her that he wanted to do more than just dance.

He moved so well, he didn't have to do anything more than dance to win her over, though. One dance with him and she was putty in his hands.

And he knew it.

And loved knowing it.

He moved with a certain swagger that she knew was justified. His confidence was one of the greatest turn-ons about him. Once a woman was in his arms there was no doubt that she was going to have a really good time. The lure of the promise was overwhelming.

So when the song ended and he said, "Let's sneak out," she didn't murmur any objection, just held on tightly to his hand and let him lead her through the crowd of beautiful people.

It amazed her that she was the one he'd chosen when he could have had any woman in the club. There were a couple of looks that asked that same question. What did she have that had attracted and besotted such a drop-dead-gorgeous man?

She didn't know. But whatever it was, she was glad she had it. Glad to be the target of envy. Glad to be leaving with the handsomest officer in the room.

He had a car waiting. It took them to the Archbishop's Mansion Inn in a quiet neighborhood of century-old houses. The opulent mansion where San Francisco's archbishop once entertained VIPs of the church was renowned for its atmosphere.

He led her to the Carmen Suite, which he'd booked because of its bathroom. In no time at all they were naked and ensconsed in the claw-footed tub, a fire blazing in the bathroom fireplace.

A bucket of champagne on ice sat by the tub, as per his instructions, and he poured them each a flute from the magnum.

He lifted his glass and clinked it against hers, toasting "To the successful wrap of *White Knight* and, more importantly, free time to spend with you, love."

She returned the toast and sipped, the bubbles tickling her nose. She hiccuped.

"Ahh, hiccups again. I know just how to cure those, remember?" he said, blowing the soapy suds until one pouty, pink nipple was exposed.

"I'm going to have to give up champagne," she said.

"What?" He lifted his head from where he'd begun the cure. "You don't like—"

"No, no. It's just that we're going to have a baby and—"

"A baby!" He threw his flute into the fire. "Why didn't you tell me?"

"I just did. I only found out this morning. And the baby is due in a few weeks over six months, the doctor thinks."

"Does that mean we can't make love?" he asked, despair in his voice.

"No. We *should* make love. A lot. In case we get a colicky baby—"

"My little girl won't get colic!"

"What makes you so sure it's going to be a little girl?"

"Because I always get what I want."

"You do, do you?"

"Got you, didn't I?"

He had. He'd gotten her, all right. She couldn't remember what her life had been like before the night Zack DeLuca asked her to dance.

"You aren't sorry, are you? I know you didn't bargain on getting a movie star."

She splashed him playfully with her cupped hand.

"Nope, just as long as I get to choose the parts, I'm a happy woman."

"You mean choose the costumes. You just want to dress me up and have your way with me. First a gunslinger, now a navy officer. What's next?"

"Your agent did send me a script about a pirate that was pretty good...."

"No, no pirates. I get seasick."

"Aw, but Zack, you'd get to wear these tall black boots and an open shirt with maybe an eye patch."

"Uh-huh, and pants so tight I can't breathe, right? I had enough of that with *Fast Draw*. No way, Victoria. Read some more scripts."

"I'm going to be too busy with the baby, so I guess you'll just have to manage your own career without any more undue influence from me. I only have one request."

"What's that, sweetheart?" he asked, pulling her into his arms.

"That you don't dance in any of your movies. Save all your dances for me."

"Great idea. Now let's dry off and do some dancing between the sheets."

MILLS & BOON®

Stories to make you smile!

Don't miss this fabulous collection of three brand new stories that will make you smile and fuel your fantasies!

Discover the fun of falling in love with these humorous stories by three romantic award-winning authors—

ELISE TITLE—ONE WAY TICKET
BARBARA BRETTON—THE MARRYING MAN
LASS SMALL—GUS IS BACK

Available from 9th March 1998 Price: £5.25

Available at most branches of WH Smith, John Menzies, Martins, Tesco, Asda and Volume One

This month's
irresistible novels from

Temptation®

CHANGE OF HEART by Janice Kaiser

It Happened One Night...

*'Twas the night before Valentine's Day...*and Liz Cabot was out celebrating her engagement with her girlfriends. She didn't expect to run into her first love, Colby Sommers. Or spend the night making mad passionate love with this heartbreaker. When she woke up the next day, who would be her valentine?

MR VALENTINE by Vicki Lewis Thompson

Jack Killigan's book had just been published but there was one hitch—his publisher thought he was a woman! After all, his novel *was* a hot, steamy romance! So Jack persuaded his childhood friend Krysta Lueckenhoff to fill in for him. Soon she's intrigued—can her old friend make love as well as he writes it?

THE GETAWAY BRIDE by Gina Wilkins

Brides on the Run

Gabe Conroy had been the happiest man in the world—until he'd returned home to find his new bride had disappeared. Devastated, he vowed he would never stop looking for her. But, once he found his runaway wife, what was he going to do with her?

RESTLESS NIGHTS by Tiffany White

Blaze

Victoria Stone had had plenty of erotic fantasies, but until she met Zack DeLuca she never imagined experiencing them for real. Not in her wildest dreams had Victoria pictured herself responding so brazenly to a perfect stranger. And it was completely crazy to go away on holiday with him...where things could only get hotter...

Spoil yourself next month
with these four novels from

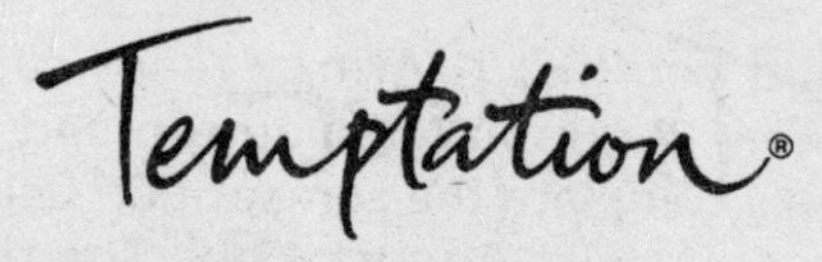

THE BLACK SHEEP by Carolyn Andrews

Nick Heagerty was a loner, a rebel *with* a cause. Ten years ago he'd been accused of a crime he didn't commit—and he'd left town without a backward glance. Now he was back—but not for long. Then *everything* changed when he met gorgeous P.I. Andie Field and realized that his wandering days were numbered...

WISHES by Rita Clay Estrada

When Virginia Gallagher found a wallet full of cash, it would've been the answer to her prayers, *if* she hadn't been so honest. When Wilder Hunnicut came to pick it up, *he* would've been a wish come true, *if* he hadn't been out of her league. And when her reward was a lamp with three wishes, she started hoping wishes really could come true...

AFTER THE LOVING by Sandy Steen

It Happened One Night

To claim her inheritance, Isabella Farentino must find a husband—fast! The only man around is the arrogant, infuriatingly sexy Cade McBride. Belle's counting on his love-and-leave-them attitude to get him out of her life, but after one incredible wedding night with Cade, she's having second thoughts...

BRIDE OVERBOARD by Heather MacAllister

Brides on the Run

Blair Thomason was about to take the plunge—into marriage, that is. But when she found herself on a yacht, about to marry a crook, she plunged into the sea instead! Luckily, Drake O'Keefe was there to rescue her... She'd barely escaped marrying one man, only to be stranded with another!

PARTY TIME!

How would you like to win a year's supply of Mills & Boon® Books? Well, you can and they're FREE! Simply complete the competition below and send it to us by 31st August 1998. The first five correct entries picked after the closing date will each win a year's subscription to the Mills & Boon series of their choice. What could be easier?

BALLOONS	BUFFET	ENTERTAIN
STREAMER	DANCING	INVITE
DRINKS	CELEBRATE	FANCY DRESS
MUSIC	PARTIES	HANGOVER

S	O	E	T	A	R	B	E	L	E	C
T	E	F	M	U	S	I	C	D	D	H
S	U	I	V	Z	T	E	Y	R	A	A
N	E	N	T	E	R	T	A	I	N	N
O	B	V	E	R	E	H	K	N	C	G
O	J	I	F	O	A	L	R	K	I	O
L	M	T	F	V	M	P	U	S	N	V
L	P	E	U	Q	E	N	Z	S	G	E
A	W	G	B	X	R	C	T	B	Y	R
B	F	A	N	C	Y	D	R	E	S	S

C8B

Please turn over for details of how to enter...

HOW TO ENTER

Can you find our twelve party words? They're all hidden somewhere in the grid. They can be read backwards, forwards, up, down or diagonally. As you find each word in the grid put a line through it. When you have completed your wordsearch, don't forget to fill in the coupon below, pop this page into an envelope and post it today—you don't even need a stamp!

Mills & Boon Party Time! Competition
FREEPOST CN81, Croydon, Surrey, CR9 3WZ
EIRE readers send competition to PO Box 4546, Dublin 24.

Please tick the series you would like to receive if you are one of the lucky winners

Presents™ ❑ Enchanted™ ❑ Medical Romance™ ❑
Historical Romance™ ❑ Temptation® ❑

Are you a Reader Service™ Subscriber? Yes ❑ No ❑

Mrs/Ms/Miss/Mr ....Intials ....
(BLOCK CAPITALS PLEASE)

Surname...

Address ....

....

.....................................Postcode.........................

(I am over 18 years of age)

C8B

One application per household. Competition open to residents of the UK and Ireland only. You may be mailed with offers from other reputable companies as a result of this application. If you would prefer not to receive such offers, please tick box. ❑

Closing date for entries is 31st August 1998.

Mills & Boon® is a registered trademark of Harlequin Mills & Boon Limited.

JANICE KAISER

Dana Kirk is a rich and successful woman, but someone wants to kill her and her teenage daughter. Who hates her enough to terrorise this single mother? Detective Mitchell Cross knows she needs help—his help—to stay alive.

"...enough plot twists and turns to delight armchair sleuths"—Publishers Weekly

1-55166-065-2
AVAILABLE FROM MARCH 1998

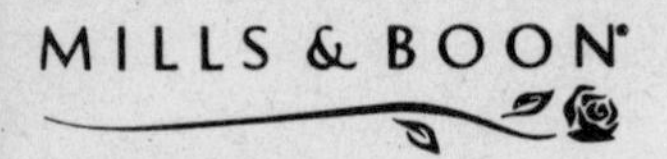

SPECIAL OFFER £5 OFF

Beautiful fresh flowers, sent by 1st class post to any UK and Eire address.

We have teamed up with Flying Flowers, UK's premier 'flowers by post' company, t offer you £5 off a choice of their two mo popular bouquets the 18 mix (CAS) of 1 multihead and 8 luxury bloom Carnation and the 25 mix (CFG) of 15 luxury bloom Carnations, 10 Freesias and Gypsophila. All bouquets contain fresh flowers 'in bu added greenery, bouquet wrap, flower fo care instructions, and personal message card. They are boxed, gift wrapped and by 1st class post.

To redeem £5 off a Flying Flowers bouq simply complete the application form be and send it with your cheque or postal to; **HMB Flying Flowers Offer, The Jersey Flower Centre, Jersey JE1**

ORDER FORM (Block capitals please) Valid for delivery anytime until 30th November 1998 MAB/01

Title .... Initials .... Surname ....

Address ....

....

.... Postcode ....

Signature .... Are you a Reader Service Subscriber Y

Bouquet(s) **18 CAS** (Usual Price £14.99) **£9.99** ☐ **25 CFG** (Usual Price £19.99) **£14.99** [

I enclose a cheque/postal order payable to Flying Flowers for £... or paym

VISA/MASTERCARD ☐☐☐☐☐☐☐☐☐☐☐☐☐☐☐☐ Expiry Date ..../........../..

PLEASE SEND MY BOUQUET TO ARRIVE BY ..../........../........

TO Title .... Initials .... Surname ....

Address ....

....

.... Postcode ....

Message (Max 10 Words) ....

....

Please allow a minimum of four working days between receipt of order and 'required by date' for de

You may be mailed with offers from other reputable companies as a result of this application.
Please tick box if you would prefer not to receive such offers. ☐

Terms and Conditions Although dispatched by 1st class post to arrive by the required date the exact day of delivery cannot be gua
Valid for delivery anytime until 30th November 1998. Maximum of 5 redemptions per household. photocopies of the voucher will be accepte